WILD HOPES

4H RANCH

EVIE MITCHELL

THUNDER THIGHS PUBLISHING

ISBN: 978-1-922561-81-7

Editor: Nicole McCurdy, Emerald Edits

 Formatted with Vellum

ACKNOWLEDGEMENT OF COUNTRY

I acknowledge the Traditional Custodians of the lands on which I write, the Ngunnawal people, and pay my respect to elders both past and present.

I acknowledge the continued and deep spiritual relationship of the Australian Aboriginal and Torres Strait Islander peoples to this land, and their unique cultural and spiritual relationships to the land, waters and seas and their rich contribution to society.

To my greedy readers,
Thank you for bringing my wild hopes to life.

And to my husband, always.

WILD HOPES

The Bad Boy Rocker meets the Mousy Girl Next Door with a STEAMY Secret...

Justice Wild tossed Peach Springs away a decade ago, leaving the town in his dust on his way to rockstar glory. Now, platinum plaques and tabloid headlines precede him, and his bad-boy persona is as electrifying as his guitar riffs. But under the leather and ink, the scars of his past run deep.

Hope Higgins, the girl next door whose apple orchard once stood proudly beside his peach, hides a secret as sweet as her pies. By day, she's a mousy virtual assistant, but by night, she's the bestselling author of a scorching hot rockstar romance series whose main character is suspiciously similar to a certain tattooed singer...

Will Hope be able to keep her secret? Or will a certain tattooed bad boy make all her dreams— including the steamy ones—come true?

Content warnings:
Discussion on page of experiencing death of parents.
Discussion of cancer diagnosis in parent and subsequent passing.
Discussion of family trauma and recovery of old relationships.
Discussion of aging grandparent and caring needs.
Discussion of grief and processing.
Experience on page of bullying allegations and public exposure.
Explicit sex scenes and sexting.

PLAYLIST

Ironic by Alanis Morrissette

9 to 5 by Dolly Parton

Hometown Glory by Adele

Free Fallin' by Tom Petty (cover by John Mayer)

Secrets by OneRepublic

Anti-hero by Taylor Swift (cover by Dermot Kennedy)

Unholy by Sam Smith and Kim Petras

Days Like This by Van Morrison (Cover by Dermot Kennedy)

Fast Car by Tracy Chapman

Say You Won't Let Go by James Arthur

Stand by Me by Ben E. King

How Do I Say Goodbye (Acoustic) by Dean Lewis

A Lot More Free by Max McNown

Beautiful Things (Acoustic) by Benson Boone
Texas Hold 'Em by Beyoncé
Body like a Backroad by Sam Hunt
Earned It by The Weeknd
If the world was ending by JP Saxe featuring Julia Michaels
Stick Season by Noah Khan
Girl Next Door by Justice Wild
Badass Woman by Megan Trainor
Photograph by Ed Sheeran
Lucky by Dermot Kennedy
Blossom by Dermot Kennedy

PROLOGUE

Hope
Three years earlier
Song: *Ironic* by Alanis Morissette

In a competition between pussy and beaver, it appeared the less hairy of the two would be triumphant

"Can I pat your beaver?"

I lumbered to turn around, mindful of the fact the tail of my costume could take out half the bar if I spun too quickly.

How did Faye talk me into this?

"Um," I mumbled, glancing around for my fellow beaver. "I don't think so."

I spotted Faye by the bar, stuck in the three-deep line waiting to order. Her back was to me, and I could see her gesticulating wildly to another customer, her black curls bouncing this way and that as she moved.

Faye! If we have a psychic connection, look at me! Now!

Alas, my best friend, also dressed as a beaver, continued to chat with the customer, who happened to be dressed as a squirrel.

"Come on," the drunk guy badgered. "It's Halloween. Let me pat your fur."

I ducked my head and turned away, hoping that if I ignored him, he'd leave me alone. Sweat poured down my back, a combination of the dancing, the costume and the man making me nervous.

"Come on. Just one little stroke." He laughed in a way that set the hairs on the back of my neck on edge. An ick feeling slithered down my spine to curl in my gut. My pulse pounded in my ears as I tried to shift away only for him to match me step for step.

"Could you please back away?" I asked, frustrated that I sounded nervous and breathy. "You're making me uncomfortable."

"Me?" The drunk seemed to be offended by my assertion. "I'm harmless."

And I'm sure that's what Hannibal Lecter said to all his victims too.

Why did men have to ruin everything?

The drunk crowded in, making a lunge for the front of my costume.

I dodged back, nearly falling over the giant claw feet shoes Faye had insisted we wear.

It'll be funny, she said. A real laugh, she said.

Why did men have to ruin everything?

"Let me pat you!" The drunk lunged again, and I fell over, tumbling onto my butt in my rush to avoid him.

He reached for me, his expression triumphant, but a stern voice snapped through the crowd, halting his movement.

"Oi!" the far too familiar voice shouted. "Get your hands off her."

I wanted the earth to swallow me up as the lead singer from the band that had just finished pushed through the crowd toward me.

Like some kind of movie hero, he slipped between me and the drunk, crossing his arms over his chest and planting his feet.

"Back up."

"But I—"

"I said," he growled. "Back the *fuck* up."

The drunk glanced around, wavering as he

eyed my rescuer—no doubt wondering if he could take him.

"Fuck it." The aggressor tossed his hands up, flicking me a furious look. "You can have her." He shoved through the crowd, disappearing into the crush.

My hero huffed. "Alright, folks. Nothing to see here."

The people with their phones turned away, returning to their conversations.

Mortified, I tried to push up from the floor only to find myself stuck. The tail made the costume butt-heavy, dragging me off-center as I tried and failed to stand.

"Here." Hands slipped under my arms, hauling me up.

And just like that I found myself in the arms of the very last person I ever thought I'd see. Faye, her brother, Trent—who was our designated driver for the evening—and I, had arrived late to the bar, and had spent most of the evening dancing at the back of the crowded room to avoid hitting people with our tails. I'd thought the singer had sounded familiar, but without hearing his name or seeing his face, I'd been left with an impression of familiarity rather than this slap in the face.

What were the chances that Justice Wild, my high school crush and main character in all of my hottest fantasies, would be performing tonight, a half a world away from Peach Springs, the small town where we'd both grown up?

My gaze traveled hungrily over him, absorbing all the changes that the last ten years had imprinted on him.

Justice had always been a good-looking kid, and unsurprisingly he'd matured into a gorgeous man. His dark brown, nearly black, hair complemented his tanned skin and green eyes. He'd grown taller since I last saw him, and based on my own short stature, I'd have pegged him as standing at an inch or so under six feet.

While his height might have changed, his enigmatic presence hadn't. His bright green eyes and his muscular body practically vibrated with barely leashed energy. Tattoos ran up and down his arms, images that had been crafted in the years since we'd last met and which meant something to him but would remain a mystery to me.

He still looked good enough to lick.

Double damn.

One would have assumed my brothers, who were still friends with him, would have mentioned it. But then no one knew about my silent obsession—and I planned to keep it that way.

"Hope?" Justice blinked, a slow smile

curving his lips. "Shit. I didn't know you were coming tonight."

My mouth opened and closed but words failed to appear. He glanced over my shoulder.

"Are your brothers here? I sent them a text but didn't hear anything back."

I shook my head. "It's picking season. They're trying to get the last fruit in before it gets too cold."

His lips twisted into a wry smile. "I should have known. What are they growing these days?"

My own curved into an answering smile. "Apples, of course. But they do have a peach orchard—just a small one."

Peach Springs, the small town where we'd both grown up, was world renowned for its peaches.... And yet my family had decided to grow apples.

These days my siblings and I lived in Capricorn Cove, a small town in the Isle of Astipia, known for its beautiful coastline and delicious fresh produce. My mother's family lived here, and she'd returned towing us kids with her after... after...

I pushed away the thought, focusing on Justice. "It's good to see you."

He grinned. "And you. Come backstage, we

can catch up. You can fill me in on what's happening in your world."

I hesitated. "My friend Faye is getting us drinks. I wouldn't want her to worry."

"Which one is she?"

I pointed at my fellow beaver and Justice barked out a laugh. "I should have known. Hey, Sam!"

Sam, the lead guitarist, glanced up from where he stood on the stage, packing up their cords and instruments.

"Can you keep an eye on Faye? Did I get her name right?"

I nodded.

"Can you let Faye—the other beaver—know I'm taking Hope backstage? We're both from Peach Springs."

Sam glanced my way, one eyebrow cocking. "You're Faye's housemate, right?"

I nodded. "And you're Sam Dogg. You live down the road."

He chuckled. "Yeah. Sorry about the noise. We try to keep it to a dull roar."

I shrugged then realized he'd never be able to see it under the heavy beaver suit. "It's not a problem. I like your stuff."

He glanced over my head at Faye, narrowing his gaze. "That's her brother, right?"

I glanced back to see she'd made it back to the table that Trent had secured and was currently gesturing wildly at him. "Yeah, that's him."

"Cool. I'll let her know where you've gone. No problem."

"Appreciate it," Justice said, catching my hand and giving me a small tug. I followed, stumbling behind him in my oversized shoes.

Seriously, why couldn't he have seen me last year? Last Halloween I dressed as Marilyn Monroe and three guys gave me their numbers.

He led me down a dark corridor behind the stage and into a small room crowded with people—all of whom stopped talking when their sexy lead singer walked in with a beaver.

God, kill me now. Please.

Justice handed me a beer and introduced me to his band and crew, whose names I promptly forgot.

"Shots?" one of the roadies asked, holding up a bottle of some clear liquid.

Justice shook his head but nodded at me. "Hope might."

I took the offered glass and downed it quickly, praying it would offer some courage—or at least dull my embarrassment.

A second shot glass replaced the first, and then a third appeared. When a fourth slipped into my hand, Justice intervened.

"How about we sit and chat for a while first?" he asked gently.

I nodded, allowing him to place a hand on my back and guide me toward a padded stool that accommodated my costume.

He took the seat next to mine, a faded armchair.

"Tell me how your family is," he encouraged.

I flapped my beaver paw, feeling a little off-center as the alcohol hit my system. "They're surviving. Capricorn Cove has been good to us. Harley, Holden and Hudson are busy with the farm."

"And Lace?" he asked, referring to my sister-in-law.

"She and Boone are great." I chuckled just thinking about my nephew. "He's growing into a temperamental teenager." My smile dipped. "But I don't know if Lace and Harley are going to last. They've had issues for a while."

"I'm sorry to hear that."

I shook my head, forcing a smile. "How about you? Tell me all about your family."

Justice blew out a breath. "I... I text them occasionally. Fletch, Beau and Asher are all still in Peach Springs. Colt got out and became a stuntman like he wanted. I see him occasionally. As for Owen...." He trailed off. "Let's just say that overall, I'm not exactly close to them anymore."

"You're estranged?"

He lifted one shoulder in a half shrug. "I don't know what we are."

I placed a furry hand on his knee. "You should fix that. Family is important—and while I'm supportive of separating from family if they're not the right people for you, I have a feeling that's not what's happening here."

He chuckled dryly. "You always know how to get to the heart of an issue."

I removed my hand reluctantly. "You should try to repair what's there. Life is too short to let wounds fester."

"I wouldn't even know where to start."

"A text to check in might be good."

He nodded thoughtfully. "I'll think on it." He shifted, changing the subject. "Alright, on to more important things. Tell me about you. What are you up to these days?"

"Study and work, that's my whole life."

He chuckled. "What? No boyfriend?"

I snorted. "No. The dating pool in this town is abysmally small. And any of the guys who might be a good match from college are either wanting to move back to the cities or run in the other direction when commitment is on the table."

I was vaguely aware that the alcohol had begun to hit me, that my hand gestures were becoming larger, and my words a little slurred.

But then, maybe it wasn't the alcohol so much as being in Justice's presence—he had such an enigmatic personality, that when he turned his full attention on you, it felt a little like floating.

A woman tripped and fell against the arm of his chair, laughing as she slid down it to land in his lap.

"Sorry!" she chuckled, her voice low and sexy. "I didn't mean to interrupt."

Justice's arms automatically wrapped around her to steady her, keeping the woman from falling.

"Not a problem. Jacie, meet Hope."

"Hey," she said brightly. "Nice to meet you."

I wasn't exactly sure which animal she was meant to be dressed as, but I made an educated guess based on the ears and whiskers that it was a cat.

A pussy cat, if you will.

And in a competition between pussy and beaver, it appeared the less hairy of the two would be triumphant.

My heart flopped sadly, an ache taking up residence in the middle of my chest as Justice allowed her to settle in his lap, leaning back against him as we chatted.

Justice wasn't for me. He never had been, and he never would be. I just needed to reconcile that my childish dreams of marrying the boy next door would never eventuate.

Thank god he'd never guessed my feelings. And, if I had it my way, he never would.

The roadie came back around and offered me another shot. I took it before Justice could stop me, needing the hit of fire to sear away the tears burning in my throat.

"Hope."

I glanced toward the door to the room and found Trent and some other guy standing in the doorway.

"You're okay," he said, his relief palatable.

Not even close.

I tilted my head to the side, offering him a blank smile. "Of course, I am. Why wouldn't I be?" I lied.

"Because you're drunk, honey." Justice tugged gently on one of my pigtails "Sounds like these nice guys are your ride home."

Don't cry, don't cry, don't cry.

I wanted to show him I could party with his crew. That I was better than the beaver costume and pigtails.

But you're not, are you? You're a small-town girl

and he's destined for stardom. The two aren't com-patible.

"But I want to—" I began.

"Time to go," Justice ordered, not brooking any protests. He shifted Jacie off his lap and stood, hauling me up once again.

"It was great seeing you, Hope," he murmured, pressing a small kiss to my forehead. "And I'll think on what you said."

An embarrassed flush crept up my neck. Once again, I wasn't anything to him.

"Off you go," Justice gave me a little shove in Trent's direction. "We'll catch up another time."

Dismissed, I ducked my head and waddled out of the room, biting the inside of my cheek hard enough to draw blood, but goddamn it, I refused to cry in front of anyone.

It was only later, in the silence of my bedroom, that I allowed the tears to come.

Next time, I promised myself. *Next time he'll see me as a woman.*

1

HOPE

Song: *9 to 5* by Dolly Parton

Give me three reasons as to why I shouldn't kill the idiots I work with.

I stared at the picture of Justice Wild hanging above my desk, mentally cataloging the ways in which he embodied the perfect bad-boy rocker vibe.

Cocky grin—check.

Tattoos—check.

Wild hair—check.

Women screaming his name—check.

Excellent music—triple check.

Once upon a time he'd lived next door. The

moody but charismatic kid who'd channeled his love of music into a billion-dollar career.

Meanwhile, here I was living in my grandmother's house, dealing with difficult employees and working for a boss that didn't seem to understand why I was stressed.

"We've never had this conversation."

I blinked as I came back to reality with a rough thud.

Taking a deep breath, I unmuted myself.

"Ciara, I don't think this is a productive meeting. You're saying we've never had this conversation before, I'm saying I've provided you with feedback both directly and through others in the team. I think—"

"The only feedback you've ever provided to me was when you called my dress attire shabby."

I stared at the woman on the other side of the screen, desperately fighting for calm.

Ciara had the potential to be an amazing employee. The issue was that she assumed she didn't need to change anything.

"I don't believe I've called your outfits shabby. That wouldn't be professional."

"You did!" Her voice caught and her eyes welled with tears. "You're a horrible boss! How can you say you didn't?"

I muted myself and stared at the screen,

biting the inside of my cheek to keep from crying. Ciara's rant began once again, her face flushing as tears ran unchecked down her cheeks.

I hated this conversation. I hated how after every catch up I felt drained and useless. I hated how this had been going on for months and despite my best efforts we seemed to be stuck in the same cycle.

I'd provide her with feedback. She'd deny I ever provided her with the feedback. I'd show her emails and notes from our meetings, and she would deny we ever had that conversation.

It had gotten to the point where I'd begun to doubt my own sanity. I'd begun to look over my notes and wonder if they were lies—figments of my imagination.

They weren't, but that was how I was beginning to feel.

An hour later the conversation ended with agreement for yet another discussion.

I ended the call and tossed off my headset, pinching the bridge of my nose to keep from crying.

"Damn it," I muttered, rolling my shoulders as if trying to shrug off the energy of the discussion we'd just had. "I don't want to do this anymore."

Once upon a time I'd loved my job. We

worked with businesses of all kinds creating custom solutions for their organizations. Be it social media posts, meeting minutes, developing project plans, or supporting staff recruitment. The work was varied and interesting, the hours were great, the pay was excellent, and I had managed a great team of twelve staff who all loved their jobs.

Or at least I had, until six months ago. Ciara had been hired and within a month my job satisfaction had deteriorated. She'd struggled to juggle clients, had refused to communicate with me what she needed, and had begun to assign her work to other team members instead of actioning herself.

I wanted to help her. I wanted her to succeed. But every effort was met with hostility and wild accusations. And my boss, George, while a good guy, didn't seem to appreciate how stressful and toxic the situation had become.

I finished up a few emails then logged off for the day as my phone beeped with an incoming text.

FAYE

Give me three reasons as to why I shouldn't kill the idiots I work with.

I grinned, leaning back in my chair as my fingers flew across the screen.

HOPE

1. You need the money. 2. You'd look horrendous in a prison outfit. 3. You're married to one of those "idiots".

FAYE

You're right. I'll add itching powder to their underwear before a gig. That'll teach 'em.

HOPE

What's happened now?

FAYE

The usual. I'm wrangling PR nightmares, Justice has gone AWOL, Felix is brooding over some couple he met on a mountain treat, Radley is being… Radley, and do NOT get me started on the sex animal I married. The man is insatiable!

HOPE

And that's a bad thing?

FAYE

It is when I'm in the middle of a call with Rolling Stone about getting them on the cover and Sam decides to crawl under my desk and eat me out.

I squealed a little, delighted my best friend in the world had landed such a good man.

We'd met in college, Faye with her bold personality and sharp wit had taken me under her wing. We'd become fast friends and quickly moved in together. We'd lived off campus in a quiet bungalow where I'd managed to kill every plant and blade of grass, and she'd managed to set fire to the cooktop three times.

After the third visit by her brother, who was a firefighter, we'd agreed that I'd take over the cooking and she could do the yard work.

I'd loved those long, busy days spent laughing over some new story or calamity. We'd been poor but happy.

Then Faye had graduated and been offered a job by The Wild Ones. Did I find it strange that Justice had employed my best friend as his PR rep? A little. But Faye had known her husband, Sam, for years before the band had formed, and Sam had suggested her when the band had needed someone passionate but cheap.

The thing I'd taken away from the whole situation is that the world is a small place.

I returned Faye's text.

HOPE

And what is the problem?

FAYE

No, you're right. Muting your
phone so you can climax is
totally professional. Thank you
for the reality check.

HOPE

This is going in a book.

FAYE

I should hope so. Speaking of…
have you seen Justice yet?

HOPE

No. Should I be expecting to?

FAYE

Maybe? He asked Simon to
organize a suit for one of his
brothers. Something about an
event coming up. Do you know
anything about that?

HOPE

You should ask him.

FAYE

I have. And the fact you're being
cryptic tells me I should push
harder before the media finds out
what's up. Thanks for nothing
you goose.

I chuckled.

HOPE

Love you too. See you in a few weeks?

FAYE

You know it!

I clicked on the after-work mode on my phone, breathing a little sigh. I missed Faye and couldn't wait to see 'her at my birthday, but there was a grief attached to seeing her moving forward with her life. A yearning I'd never expected had begun to take root in my chest—a wish for the kind of things she had.

I wanted her to be happy and fulfilled more than I wanted my next breath. My heart held such joy for her—she deserved every good thing. But watching her find her dream job, travel the world, embrace herself, and find a relationship with a person who adored and complemented her in every way, made me want the same.

I'm lonely.

I didn't have any problem with being single —in fact most of my life I'd preferred it. But lately my world had narrowed to become one video call, text or email after another. My friends were moving on with their lives while I felt... stuck.

I loved my gran, but she had become the

only person I physically interacted with. I longed for connection, meaning, touch. I knew I needed to crack the shell I'd built around my life, but I'd become trapped, like a wallflower or bluestocking that had a badge placed upon her before she'd even fully matured.

"Get over yourself." I forced away my morose thoughts and opened my personal laptop. "Your life is fine."

Flexing my fingers as my manuscript loaded, I glanced up at the picture of Justice hanging above my desk.

"Let's see what mischief you're getting up to tonight."

By day I was Hope Higgins, the shy virtual assistant who lived with her grandmother and made pies for the town charity events.

But by night I was H. Stone, author of the bestselling series, "Savage." The series followed the sexual exploits of the Savage Boys, a band that had taken the world by storm. The books featured each of the band members as they fell in love and found their soul mate.

It was the worst-kept secret that Justin Savage, my lead character, was inspired in no small part by Justice Wild.

Did I have a crush?

Oh yeah.

But I'd been nursing that sucker since I was

four years old and Justice had agreed to push me on a swing.

Would my dream of being the woman he came home to each night ever come true?

Absolutely not.

Would my dream of some epic love filled with steamy sex and deliciously delightful public declarations of love ever come true?

Again, no.

One could say I wasn't exactly the kind of woman who inspired feelings of love and devotion in others. I'd once been referred to as a wallflower by a well-meaning but horrendously insensitive aunt.

My books had become an outlet for my unfulfilled desires. Every night I wrote about all the things I wished would happen in my life knowing none of it was even remotely close to reality. For brief periods I could be someone else—someone bold and confident. Someone who inspired love and lust and devotion.

Someone who wasn't lonely.

"Hope, dinner's ready."

I hit save and sat back in my chair, stretching my arms and cracking my back.

My family had no idea I wrote smutty romance, and I intended to keep it that way.

I headed downstairs, pausing when I saw

my grandmother sitting outside on the back deck.

"Gran?"

She waved at me through the porch door. "Come sit with me, dear. I have news."

"News" always translated to gossip—and as the oldest member of our small town of Peach Springs, Gran always seemed to know everything about everyone.

I served myself up a plate of chicken and salad and settled beside her on the porch swing.

"First, I heard from Hudson today," she said, referring to my youngest brother.

"How is he?"

"He and Natalie are thinking of enrolling Remy in dance classes next fall."

I chuckled. "I can't imagine Hudson as a dance dad."

"Mr. Allen from Peach Fuzz also called today." Mr. Allen had owned the local barber shop for more years that I'd been alive.

"Mm?" I murmured as I chewed. My attention had begun to drift back to the story that awaited me upstairs.

Maybe I could have Justin meet his potential match at a—

"Justice Wild is back in town."

My attention diverted so quickly I was surprised I didn't end up with whiplash.

"What?"

Gran nodded, spearing a cherry tomato with her fork. "The boy is back in town. Went to the Fuzz for a haircut. Tipped Mr. Allen good, too. Must be here for the dedication."

I swallowed then swallowed again, fighting against the rolling emotions that had spontaneously erupted in my gut.

"Dedication?"

"The court case was finally settled. The developer lost. The park is safe. It'll be handed over to the town officially in a few weeks. Didn't you read the paper?"

I shook my head slowly, trying to piece together my thoughts.

Twenty years ago, Justice's parents had been working to donate a large tract of their land to the town. They'd been peach farmers— and while the rest of their land had been perfect for agricultural use, that area was far too rocky and hilly for them to utilize.

They'd decided to donate it as a nature reserve to the town for everyone to use. Only they'd passed away before finalizing the donation, and a developer had lodged an appeal with the town to try and get the area rezoned for housing.

"I must have missed the news."

"Well, you've been on that computer for

weeks. Barely leaving the house, working around the clock." Gran tsked under her breath. "You're letting your life roll by without participating in it."

I brushed away her concerns. "Why is Justice in town? I thought he was on his tour."

Gran waved her hand dismissively. "The tour is on break for two months before the next leg. Word has it he caught some kind of cold." She sniffed. "Gladys is sure it's mono."

"And he's spending it here? In town?"

Gran nodded.

I swallowed, glancing away as I stared out at the apple trees that surrounded our small cottage.

Unlike the rest of the town, which was peach obsessed, my great-great-great-great grandparents had decided to plant apples.

Apples had been my family's obsession until my father had passed away when I was thirteen. My mother had tried to continue the tradition and run the orchard, but her heart hadn't been in it. A few years later she'd moved us halfway across the world back to her home country of Astipia.

My father's side of the family still ran the orchard, which was well known for its fresh, crisp varieties of heirloom, organic fruit.

That was why I was here. My Gran—my father's mother—needed help around the house while she waited for a spot to open at the local assisted living home. But with peak fruit picking season nearly upon us, there wasn't anyone in the family who could assist her.

And so, I'd upended my life, moved halfway around the world and returned to Peach Springs to help.

The adjustment hadn't been easy. Being an apple in a town full of peaches had its downsides. Not to mention being the only member of my family who lacked a green thumb. I couldn't even keep a succulent alive, let alone an apple tree. Thankfully no one seemed to expect me to pitch in on the farming side.

"I want you to take that pie you baked this morning over to the Wild house."

My head twisted to stare at my tiny, wrinkled grandmother. Her dark black hair had faded to a striking white. We shared the same blue eyes, though hers were a much deeper blue than my own. Unlike shy me with my average height, abundant hips and overly generous breasts, her small frame and petite body belied her larger-than-life personality. She had ruled her home with an iron fist—and all her children still bowed to her whims.

I aspired to be my gran when I grew up.

"But that was for our dessert."

Gran pegged me with a glare that said southern hospitality was alive and damn near considered sacred by her.

"You make sure you take the cream I just made too," she said, ignoring my protest.

"Yes, ma'am." I bowed my head, pushing absently at the salad on my plate.

"You're a good girl, Hope." Gran pat my leg. "Now go put on a nice dress. You never know, maybe one of those Wild boys will take a liking to you."

I snorted.

She tsked gently once again. "Stranger things have happened."

Yeah, right.

2

JUSTICE

Song: *Hometown Glory* by Adele

***The return of the prodigal son was less than
enthusiastic***

I leaned against my rented truck and stared up at the old farmhouse, fighting to catalog the complexity of emotions that rolled through me.

Damn, not much had changed.

And yet everything had.

Or maybe not everything so much as me.

"Fuck," I muttered, running a hand through my freshly cut hair. "That's far too deep for this time of the evening."

I'd delayed the inevitable family reunion for as long as possible by working my way from one side of town to the other. I didn't mind spending money in the small businesses that lined Main Street, but at some point, the businesses had ended, and I'd been forced to face reality.

Fuck.

I moved to push off the truck but movement from across the yard caught my attention. I squinted into the setting light, struck by the flame-colored locks highlighted by the fading sun, and a round dish in one hand. Whoever she was, the woman had the body of Venus— and those legs?

I needed them wrapped around me.

"Justice?"

My filthy thoughts screeched to a halt.

I raised my arm to squint into the light.

"Hope?"

She nodded, stepping into the shadow of the house. "I thought that was you."

My brain struggled to reconcile the woman before me with the feelings of almost sisterly love I had for her.

"Hope Higgins. I haven't seen you since...." I trailed off as a grin tugged at my lips.

She waved one hand dismissively. "We don't have to talk about that."

The last time I'd seen her had been in some

dive bar in a little coastal town where my lead guitarist, Sam, hailed from. It'd been Halloween, and while most women had been dressed to kill, Hope had chosen a beaver costume—a big brown thing with giant feet, fake claws, and a thick tail. She'd made me laugh that night—and damn had I needed the distraction. But then she always had been able to make me smile.

I sobered, remembering the fucker that had attempted to accost her that night. The bastard had deserved more than a warning—but I'd promised to be on my best behavior and had fought off the urge to lay him out.

I crossed my arms and tucked one leg over the other as I leaned against my truck. "I don't know about that, darlin'," I drawled slowly, enjoying watching her squirm. "It's not every day a woman shows me her beaver."

Even in the dim evening light I could see the red flush creeping from under her primly buttoned cardigan.

I found myself strangely intrigued by the idea of slipping those buttons free just to see how far that blush slipped down her skin.

I shook off the thought. Hope Higgins had always been the good girl next door. Quiet, dutiful, and shy. All through school she'd volunteered for all the shit that people should care about but rarely do—like raising money to save the whales or encouraging people to recycle.

I eyed her, quietly pleased to see she still wore button-up cardigans and her hair in braids.

Though my fingers itched to release her hair from its current braid, which looked far too tight for a woman whose face deserved to be on the cover of magazines. Because Hope Higgins, despite her best efforts to downplay her charms, was a bombshell.

If she'd been anyone else, I might have been tempted to do more than tease her. But this was Hope—the good girl next door. As I'd been told more times than I could count, good girls deserved great guys and I wasn't anywhere close to being a good guy.

Mentally, I chastised my dick for wanting her.

We're not even close to being in her league.

"It was a costume." Hope's chin jutted out stubbornly. "A lot of people dress as beavers for Halloween."

"Name one."

"Faye."

I shook my head. "Doesn't count. Faye is a maniac."

"Hey! She's my best friend."

I grinned. "I won't hold that against you."

Her gaze narrowed, amusement dancing in their glorious depths. "You're one to talk. Didn't some woman burn your clothes the other week?"

I winced. "I will neither confirm nor deny."

"Hmm, hedging your bets."

"What can I say, I'm a gambler." I eyed the pie in her hands. "Speaking of, if I was a betting man, I'd assume that might be for me."

"Don't count on it." She held the pie away. "This is for Asher."

"Bullshit. Why'd you bring that grump a treat?"

"Your brother is a good guy. Last week he helped Gran to our car after she got tired in the grocery store."

"He's a saint. I'll be sure to nominate him for a medal."

She snorted, juggling the pie pan from one hand to the other. "You're a smartass, you know that, right?"

I chuckled, appreciating her sass. The Hope I'd known from years past had been shy and reserved, sweet with a cracking sense of humor. This Hope had all the same traits—but with a confidence and maturity that I found sexy as hell.

Not in her league, remember?

"Justice? That you?"

I stiffened, dread settling like a stone in my stomach. "Hello, Asher."

The light from the porch bathed my brother in a soft glow. He'd aged since I'd last been home, his brown hair now holding some salt near his temples. His skin would always be tanned—it was the kind of bone-deep color that came from decades of farming under the warm sun.

He looked so much like our dad it hurt to see him.

"The prodigal son returns," Asher said, his tone dry.

It appeared that unlike the rest of the town, my reception at home would be less than enthusiastic.

But then what did I expect? I hadn't exactly left under the most auspicious of circumstances.

In fact, if memory served me right, I might have told everyone in my family to make enthusiastic love to themselves as I tossed my gear in my truck and drove off in a fit of egotistical rage.

It had worked out. Being alone had forced me to grow up. I'd worked my ass off to prove my brothers wrong about pursuing a career in music.

Now here I stood, an international rockstar with more money than a man could spend in a lifetime, owning five properties and numerous awards, and adored by fans the world over.

And somehow driving through the gates of the farm had transported me back to the exact maturity level of that angry 20-year-old.

My jaw tightened, my hands curling into fists as we stared each other down.

Hope thrust the pie dish into my hands as she shifted between us, grinning widely at Asher.

"Gran sent me," she said, walking away from me and up to the porch. "Said I should bring over a pie since you'll soon have a full house on your hands."

My gaze dropped to her ass before snapping back up.

She's like a little sister. Jesus, man, get your shit together.

Asher softened, greeting Hope with the same warmth that she seemed to bring out in everyone she met.

I didn't know how but within a few sentences she'd broken the ice between me and my brother, smoothing over our rough edges.

She bustled inside the old farmhouse, acting for all the world like she owned it.

"Is Madilyn in?" she asked as she walked down the hall, Asher and me trailing her like lost ducklings.

"No, she's down at the Pink Peach," Asher answered, referring to the local hair salon.

Hope nodded, making her way to the kitchen. "Coffee or tea?"

It appeared that she was staying—at least for the moment.

Thank god.

I popped the pie on the old kitchen table and took in the changes in the old house. Much remained the same, like the battered wood chopping block and height markers that Mom and Dad had etched into the doorway as we grew. But other things were different—the cabinets had been brightened with a new coat of paint, and the appliances had been updated.

"Nothing for me," I muttered, taking my place at the ancient wooden table. My fingers automatically wandered across the surface, finding the worn creases and cracks in the wood.

"Coffee, thanks," Asher muttered, taking his own seat across from me.

Old habits died hard it seemed, as we sat in the same places we'd occupied throughout our growing years.

Hope chattered in the background as she bustled around the kitchen, her voice a pleasant distraction from the emotions rolling through me.

Her ease in the kitchen indicated a familiarity that I wasn't sure I liked. I eyed my brother, wondering what the relationship between them could be. Were they friends? Former lovers?

My jaw clenched at the thought of Asher with Hope. She deserved a guy who'd show her the world, not some grumpy bastard who needed to be put in his place regularly.

It's why he and Madilyn worked—she understood him.

"You staying here?" Asher asked when there was a brief lull.

I shrugged. "Maybe just for a night or two, if you can find a space for me."

He nodded, accepting a mug from Hope. "You can have your old room. The bed's still in there but Madilyn's converted it into a guest room."

Hope slid a cup in front of me.

"I said—"

"Drink," she ordered, giving me a meaningful look. "Please."

I swallowed my protest and raised the mug to my lips. The fruity flavor of the hot liquid exploded on my tongue and sent me spiraling. I glanced at Hope who shot me a small smile then ducked her head, hiding her expression behind a wall of hair.

Peach tea had been my mom's favorite. She'd always loved to make it for us on cool evenings as a reminder that summer would soon come.

The last time I'd tasted it had been after the funeral. Hope had handed me a thermos full of the sweet tea, telling me I deserved to remember the good before the bad.

My chest tightened as I took another sip, savoring the sweet brew.

Hope retrieved a knife to slice thick wedges of pie, sliding them onto plates that I didn't recognize.

Yet another thing that's changed.

"So," Asher said, breaking the silence. "You sticking around for a while?"

I shrugged. "Depends if I can find a house."

Hope's eyebrows rose. "A house?"

I nodded, accepting her pie offering. "I need a base while I'm here. The band will be flying in and out to collaborate on our next album, and we need to practice ahead of the next leg of the tour."

Asher frowned into his coffee, not saying a word.

Well, this is awkward.

Sure, I hadn't seen my brothers in person for several years, but I'd kept in touch with the occasional text or phone call. I wasn't a complete ass.

Hope made eyes at me over her mug, jerking her head toward Asher in a not-so-subtle gesture.

Swallowing a grin at her antics, I cleared my throat.

"I thought Beau and Fletch might be here."

Asher shook his head. "Fletch has a shift and Beau is… god only knows where Beau is."

I relaxed slightly. "Still giving you trouble, huh?"

My brother blew out a breath, running his hand through his hair. "I'm ready to give up."

Like you did with me? I wanted to ask but bit my tongue.

"How's work?" Asher asked Hope. "That woman still giving you trouble?"

She huffed out a small chuckle. "Let me guess, Gran told you?"

"She told Madilyn who told me."

I frowned as I speared a piece of pie. "Someone's giving you trouble?"

Hope shook her head. "It's nothing. Or at least it's not that big a deal."

"No?" Asher asked. "Way your gran relayed it, seems like it is."

Hope dipped her head. "It'll be fine. Everything will work out."

"You don't sound sure," I said, watching her closely.

"It's...." Her smile seemed forced. "It is what it is. I can't change it at the moment, but it will all fix itself soon."

"You need someone to intervene?" I asked, already feeling my blood pressure rising at the thought of someone fucking with Hope.

Her body language shifted, hunching over and turning away. "No. It's fine."

She'd said "fine" far too many times in a row for it to be so, but I accepted her hint to change the subject, making a mental note to ask Asher about it later.

I pointed at the untouched pie on her plate. "Eat your gran's gift. Everything will taste better."

A genuine smile graced her lips. "Actually, that's my recipe."

"Marry me."

Her smile froze, her eyes widening before red surged into her cheeks. "No, thank you," she replied primly. "I don't think we'd be compatible."

"That's true," Asher said, nursing his coffee. "Justice would ruin a sweet girl like you."

I leaned back in my chair, trying to keep the bitterness out of my tone. "You think? Maybe Hope wouldn't mind a walk on the wild side."

Asher's jaw clenched—the expression far too familiar. "Look here, Justice. You've been gone a long time and I won't have you—"

Abruptly Hope pushed up from the table, coughing and spluttering as she did so. "I have to—that is—I mean—I need to—Gran will be expecting—"

Before I could apologize for the sibling minefield I'd lobbed her into, she'd grabbed her bag and had run for the door, disappearing into the evening light.

"Fuck," I muttered, pushing up from my seat, already regretting my actions.

Asher sighed. "We were both asses. You gonna chase after her?"

"I'm not a dick, Asher. Someone has to make sure she gets home okay."

His gaze pierced mine, some unidentifiable emotion crossed his face before I could categorize it. "It's a five-minute walk on a well-used path."

I shot him a glare over my shoulder. "If Hope were Madilyn, would you—"

He waved me off. "Fine. But at least apologize to her while you're at it. From the both of us. She didn't need to be brought into our shit."

Our shit? You're the one who started it.

You'd have thought nearly a decade away

would have broken me of the near-compulsive need I had to prove my brother wrong.

A maddening itch started on the back of my neck. "I know. I'll make it right."

"Good." Asher turned back to his pie. "I'll try to hide your slice from Beau but no promises. The boy has a sixth sense when it comes to free food."

3

HOPE

Song: *Free Fallin'* by Tom Petty (cover by John Mayer)

Turns out you can't die from humiliation

"**G**od, please, strike me down," I begged as I hurried back to Gran's.

I'd known that Justice was joking, but damn if his joke hadn't hit straight to the core of my desires.

Marry me.

I swear my heart had seized in my chest when Justice had uttered those words.

"Stupid, stupid, stupid!"

My cheeks were on fire, and my hands trembled as I stumbled down the path between our houses. The trees around me stood silent, no doubt judging me.

Don't worry, I judge myself.

I leaned over, huffing out a breath.

"Stupid!"

My stomach churned as my brain replayed my reaction to Justice's teasing again and again.

I need to move to Peru or Papua New Guinea. Somewhere remote with little access to the internet. I can't believe I acted that way—who am I?

I stumbled in the dark, nearly tripping on the loose gravel.

"Oh no." I groaned, catching myself. "The pie dish."

I'd really liked that dish too, but such was the sacrifice I was willing to make to avoid seeing either brother ever again.

I let out a small groan, scrubbing a hand over my face. "Why is it that any time I'm in Justice's presence I act like a teenager rather than a woman? What am I, fourteen? Ugh!"

My crush on Justice had been formed years before he'd become famous, but it had been during the hard years that it had solidified. During the years when my dad had been sick, the cancer slowly eroding his strength until there had been nothing left but the twinkle of the man I'd known.

I swiped angrily at the tears that filled my eyes, determined not to cry over the memories.

My father's death had come two years after his diagnosis. It had been hard on my entire family—my three brothers had changed, becoming moody or overly protective of our family. My mother had lost weight, her usually cheerful disposition slowly vanishing until all that remained was a fake smile and empty words.

We'd celebrated life and the small moments throughout his illness, but everything had been tainted by the knowledge that this first would be his last.

My eldest brother, Harley, had gotten his teenage girlfriend pregnant, gifting Dad his first grandchild—and the only one he'd lived to meet.

My middle brother, Holden, had learned the art of the wisecrack, turning into a sullen and moody beast of a boy, sneaking out at night to get into all sorts of mischief.

Meanwhile, my youngest brother, Hudson, had lived to please. He'd become mine and my mother's keeper, making us smile and taking care of the both of us.

And I, as the youngest of all my siblings, had retreated into the pages of my books, encouraged by my dad to read his favorites before visiting the hospice care where we'd discuss the intricacies of each storyline.

He'd been the one to encourage me to write—to find an escape. He'd also been the one to hand me my first notebook and a fancy, engraved fountain pen.

"Write," he'd said to me. "Give voice to your dreams, Hope. That's all any of us can do."

And so, I'd written about the boy next door.

The boy who snuck a drunk Holden through my bedroom window more nights than I could count while Mom slept downstairs.

The boy who'd wink at me during church prayers when all I'd wanted to do was scream at the injustice of losing a parent I loved.

The boy who handed me daisies when I was sad and forced me to laugh when I wanted to cry.

The boy who looked out for me in the schoolyard when the other girls were horrid because I was the one wearing my brothers' hand-me-downs because my family couldn't afford both new clothes and medical bills.

The boy who'd bought me ribbons for my hair for my birthday, and pink ink for my pen at Christmas.

Justice had been the light I'd needed when my life had been shrouded in darkness.

When his parents had died, I'd tried to return the favor, offering him a shoulder to cry on and leaving childish things for him to find that I knew would make him laugh.

There'd been a brief moment when I'd thought we might have been shaping our relationship into something more—something less "best friend's little sister" and more "woman I want to spend my life with." But that had been wishful thinking on my part, and before I could reconcile my reality with my dreams, Mom had decided to return to her home country to live near her family. That had been it—the end of whatever might have been.

But it hadn't been the end. I'd continued to write about Justice until my words had become stories and those stories had become books.

And now I was living in a nightmare of my own creation because ultimately Justice wasn't the problem—I was. He'd never done anything to deserve the reaction I'd thrown at him tonight.

"Blast," I muttered as I not-so-quietly stomped my way up the front steps of Gran's house. "I'm going to have to apologize."

I shoved open the door only to see that Gran was on the telephone—no doubt speaking to one of her many friends from across town.

The local rumor mill thrived thanks to my grandmother. I didn't want to brag, but if gossip were an Olympic sport, Gran would be the GOAT.

She raised her hand in welcome and I waved back but didn't stop. I needed to get back to a world where I was in control.

I took the stairs two at a time, rushing up the familiar hall and into the ancient bedroom only to skid to a halt—my heart slamming into my chest.

"Justice?"

He turned slowly away from the poster on my wall that he'd been staring at to cock an eyebrow at me. "This room needs an update."

Heat burst across my cheeks and down my neck. "I haven't exactly had time. And how exactly did you get here?"

"I took the shortcut."

I frowned. "There's a shortcut?"

"Yeah, through the bull paddock. You just have to run really fast."

I wasn't sure if I should be flattered or terrified that a man worth more than my entire family's income combined was risking his neck to climb in my bedroom window.

He gestured at the giant king bed that took up the majority of the space. The bed itself had been made by my great-great-grandfather, and most of the bedding looked to have come from around the same time period.

"Please tell me that mattress is from this century."

I grimaced. "I wish."

He shook his head. "And the fringe on the blankets? That can't be comfortable."

I felt myself relaxing a little at his teasing. "It's not."

"Why not change it? You've been here for how long exactly?"

"Five months." I walked over to touch one of the hand-stitched throw pillows that sat unused on the bedding box at the foot of the bed. "I want to but...." I paused, trying to find the words to make him understand.

"But?" he prompted when I didn't say anything.

I swallowed against the disloyal lump that had formed in my throat. "Don't tell Gran, but I feel like if I make this bedroom mine—if I change anything no matter how small—then it means I'm staying. And I'm not sure I want to stay."

He nodded, seemingly absorbing my words without judgment.

"It feels... awful to admit that." I sighed, flopping down to sit on the bed. "But it's the truth. I don't know if this is the place for me."

"I get it." Justice grabbed my desk chair and straddled it, crossing his arms across the back of the seat. "Being back is rough. Everything is at once familiar and yet..."

I grinned ruefully. "'And yet' is correct."

We fell into a comfortable silence, though we both avoided eye contact.

Time to woman up and get over this awkwardness.

"Justice, I—"

"Hope, I'm—"

We laughed, the tension breaking.

"You first," I said, gesturing at him.

"I'm sorry for tonight. You were trying to make things easier for me and Asher, and I fucked up."

I shook my head emphatically. "No. You were kidding around. My reaction wasn't—that is to say—I mean..." I cleared my throat. "My reaction was inappropriate." I cast out, desperate for some reason to justify my reaction. "It's just that Gran was on my case earlier tonight about dating and, well, I was already feeling a little raw over my single status."

Justice frowned. Our gazes met and he looked to be searching for something. "Being single isn't a bad thing."

"It is when everyone treats you like their little sister rather than a fuckable woman." I slapped my hand over my mouth. "Damn! What is it about you that makes me say inappropriate things?"

He grinned, seemingly pleased by my admission. "Don't hold back on my account."

I threw a pillow at him in response.

He easily caught it and tossed it back, managing to land it in my lap.

"You're really trying to tell me that the men around here aren't knocking down your door?" he asked.

I didn't want to be having this conversation with a man who had dated some of the most beautiful people in the world.

I half-shrugged. "No one is. Not here, not back home, not in any place I've ever been."

"Come on," he teased. "You're gorgeous."

I grimaced. "Thanks, but I can assure you there's no one."

"What are you trying to say?"

I hesitated, embarrassed to admit my inexperience to this rock god. Surely, I'd experienced enough embarrassment and shame for one night.

"There's never been anyone... if you catch my drift."

"So, you're...." He hesitated. "I hate the word 'virgin' because, let's be honest, virginity is a social construct."

I rolled my eyes.

"But let's go with 'abstinent'. Are you abstinent?"

I cringed. "Not by choice."

Justice remained silent, waiting for me to continue.

"It's pitiful, right? In this day and age of apps and online dating and reality TV, I really should have been able to find someone who wanted to be with me for longer than five minutes. But that's not what happened. And as I got older it just seemed like all the good guys were in relationships and the leftovers were... well, left behind for a reason."

I couldn't quite believe the words that were coming out of my mouth, but once the tap had been turned on, it appeared it wasn't likely to stop anytime soon.

"I mean," I continued, waving a hand around to emphasize my point. "It's almost like men can smell the inexperience on me. As soon as I'm in a room with a date, they switch from interested to 'can I introduce you to my mother? She'd love to have you at church on Sunday.' It's never, 'let me bend you over the table and fuck you until you're screaming my name.'" I began to pace, my hands gesturing wildly. "And I don't understand why. It's not as if I'm rude or have some kind of communicable disease like covid or something. I'm just a woman in her prime who wants great sex. Is that too much to ask? That someone brings me to climax at least three times before they—"

Justice made a sound in the back of his throat, interrupting my monologue of singledom woes.

"Too much?" I asked, wincing.

"Um, no?"

I blew out a breath. "What I'm trying to say is that men and I don't mix."

He frowned. "I don't believe that."

I gestured to my body. "I mean look at me."

"I am."

The gravity in his voice broke through the self-pity that had descended.

He cleared his throat. "I'm going to say this as a man who loves women and as your friend."

"Are we friends?" I asked quietly.

He ignored me. "You are sexy, Hope. You've got this quiet beauty which you subdue behind cute outfits and button-up cardigans. But—and I say this not to embarrass you but to reassure you—those outfits drive a guy crazy. It makes us want to peel off the layers and see what you're wearing underneath. It makes us want to work out if you're a librarian on the streets and a freak in the sheets."

My heart flip-flopped wildly as a warm, pleasant ache began to throb deep in my belly.

He thinks I'm sexy.

I brushed off the compliment. "The evidence says otherwise."

His grin was slow and sweet like honey. "You don't believe me."

"No one has ever said anything like this to me. Or indicated even a word of that might be true." I crossed my arms over my chest, determined to protect my heart.

"Sweetheart, you're hanging out with the wrong kind of men."

I rolled my eyes. "You know where I can find the right kind of guy?"

"Nope," he answered cheerfully. "But you'll know it when you find him."

"And how exactly will I know?"

"He'll be the guy who makes you realize that there's nothing wrong with being inexperienced. You're a vibrant woman, Hope. Your sexuality and sexual experience are only one part of the richness of your life. If you wanted to go out and experience sex, all you'd need to do is wear a tight red dress and some cowboy boots down to the bar. Believe me, every punk farmer and cowboy blow-in would be drooling to take what you offered." He stood up from his seat, stepping toward the window. "But that's not who you are. You want the candles and rose petals and the silk sheets."

I frowned, frustrated by his assumption.

"How do you know that?" I asked. "I'm not sixteen, and this isn't a Christmas movie."

He plucked a book off my shelf and my heart dropped.

"Because you read these."

It was the first in my rockstar romance series. The cover looked innocent with the image of drumsticks laying across a bed, but the interior was filled with all the filthy longings of my heart.

Let's just say my vibrator and I had gotten intimately acquainted while writing that book and waiting for Mr. Right.

A boldness prompted by years of people—men—assuming they knew best, possessed me. I stormed across my room to him and picked up three of my books, shoving them into his chest.

"Before you judge me for loving romance how about you read what I might enjoy?"

I forced myself to meet his surprised gaze, pleased as punch to see a new glint of interest in his expression.

"You never know," I said snottily. "You might learn a thing or two about what a woman *actually* wants."

His grin sent butterflies fluttering in my belly.

"Now go," I said, turning him around and

pushing him toward the window. "Before Gran wonders if I've really lost all my senses."

"Can't I use the front door?"

"Did you use it coming in?"

"No."

"Then no. Not if you don't want to have the story sold to the papers within an hour."

Justice froze and I crashed into his back.

"Actually," he said with a slow drawl. "That's not a half-bad idea."

"What?"

He nodded as if to himself. "What are you doing tomorrow?"

"Working. Like I always do. Why?"

"You free for brunch?"

I hesitated, unsure of where he was going with this. "Maybe."

"Meet me at the diner. I have a proposition for you."

And on that ominous note, the boy next door climbed out my bedroom window and disappeared into the cool night.

"What in the butthole of the world just happened?" I muttered.

I moved to my computer and froze when I registered that his picture was missing.

Turns out you can't die from humiliation, even if you wish otherwise.

4

JUSTICE

Song: *Secrets* by OneRepublic

I never joke about women's empowerment

In this town, peaches ruled all decisions. There wasn't anywhere you could go without having peaches thrown in your face.

Candles? Peach scents.

Hair salon? Peach shampoo.

The local diner? Peach pancakes.

Living here, I'd never noticed the zeal with which people pushed their peach-y wares. There were peach-themed ceramics, peach-pun shirts, peach desserts at the bakery and peach preserves at the local store.

Which made Hope's family an anomaly in this town.

Damn, just thinking about apples made me think about Hope and the startling conversation we'd had last night. Who would have thought the shy girl next door had a naughty side?

I mean, I did. But then I'm a degenerate asshole. I assume that everyone is as fucked up as me.

I glanced around, catching sight of my security detail in booths around the diner. The guys were discreet, attempting to grant me the façade of privacy if not the reality.

Sighing, I glanced back down at my phone, absently clicking into the notes app to jot some lyrics that had been playing through my mind all night.

I'd been intrigued by Hope's boldness and sass as she'd ordered me to read the books that had lined her shelves.

I'd made assumptions about them—and about her. Turned out my girl didn't want soft and slow. She wanted filthy, dirty, needy sex.

And the fuck if that didn't turn me on.

My girl?

I stiffened.

Shit. When had I begun to think of her as mine? I didn't. I couldn't. She had to remain the girl next door. She had to remain my friend's sister.

Besides, no way would she let me touch her. She had too much self-respect to roll in the hay with a guy like me.

The bell above the door jingled, and like clockwork, Hope stepped into the diner.

She wore a pretty blue dress with a white cardigan. Her auburn hair had been pulled back from her face by a hair ribbon that appeared to be failing, allowing wisps of hair to curl around her face.

Sweet and sexy, just looking at her felt at once familiar and new. A dichotomy I didn't know how to interpret.

Taking a seat across the booth, Hope flicked open her menu and lifted it in front of her face, examining the faded writing as if it held the answers to the universe.

I grinned, already knowing her order. It'd been the same every weekend when Harley, Holden and Hudson took her here for a meal. We'd all pile into the booth, sharing laughs and teasing, bumping elbows as we'd picked from each other's plates. There'd always been a riot of kids and teens when we'd come, and my brothers and I had been leaders of our rambunctious pack.

A strange hollow feeling took up residence in my chest. I rubbed it absently as I watched Hope make her decision.

Ruby, one of the waitresses, made her way over.

"Well if it isn't the wildest of the Wild boys," she said, slapping a hand on her hip saucily. The woman couldn't be a day under seventy, but she worked her age like she worked her sass for tips. She still dyed her hair a fire-engine red and still painted her lips and nails to match. She'd developed more wrinkles since the last time I'd seen her, but her piercing brown eyes hadn't dulled one bit.

"Ms. Ruby," I greeted with a slow, easy smile. "How you been?"

She waved me off. "Nothing changes around here." She tilted her head toward the door where a flood of paparazzi hovered outside. "Except that, apparently."

They'd arrived in the night like assassins, camping out at the end of our drive to try and snap pictures of the rockstar returning to his roots.

They came with the territory, and while I'd become used to them, I couldn't say I enjoyed any aspect of the vulture-like mob.

"Ignore them," I said, forcing my smile to

stay on my face. "Or better yet, take 'em all a piece of pie and charge it to me."

"They don't deserve our pie," Ruby said with a sniff. "Now, am I getting you both the usual?"

I nodded, waiting until Hope finally dropped her menu on the table.

"Yes please," she said, still avoiding eye contact with me. "And a milkshake, thank you."

"One day, Hope Higgins, you'll surprise me," Ruby said, waggling her pencil at her.

Hope grinned for the first time since sitting down. "I doubt that very much."

"You never know."

Ruby left us alone and I spread out, stretching an arm across the back of the booth as I watched her do everything within her power to ignore me.

"I started reading your books."

Her head flew up, her eyes wide as she stared at me. "You—my—"

"Yeah." I dropped my voice, forcing her to lean in to hear me. "They're hot. Didn't think you were into that kind of thing."

I delighted in the blush that flamed across her face. "I like it."

Her mouth opened and shut a few times before she finally summoned words. "I told you."

I chuckled, leaning back in my seat. "So, you did."

"Which book are you reading?"

"The first one about the drummer. Though I have to say, I might need to track down this H. Stone woman. Not to come across as a diva or anything—"

"Never," Hope said with a straight face.

"But Justin, the lead singer? The way he's described, and some of the things he does...." I ran a hand over my face. "Well, it cuts a little close to home."

Hope frowned. "You think so?"

I rolled back the sleeve of my Henley to bare my forearm, turning it so she could see my dagger tattoo. It read "half agony, half hope" on each side of the blade—a nod to my mother's favorite book. The dagger itself pierced a peach —a nod to my father.

"I'd think this is a bit of a unique tattoo."

She nodded and swallowed rapidly, her gaze glued to my forearm. "Yes, I suppose it is."

"And this?" I pulled my shirt up to reveal my chest tattoo—a giant dragon, with the dragon wrapping itself around my biceps, triceps and across my chest.

I watched as Hope's gaze heated, growing distant as she stared at my chest.

"I... I never really considered it before," she

murmured. "But tattoos don't necessarily equate to a stolen likeness."

I moved to drop my shirt, but her next question stopped me.

"Why do you have a blank spot on your chest?" she asked, fiddling with her napkin.

I laid my hand over the naked skin, watching her for signs of judgment. "It's for the woman I'll spend my life with. I want her to be inked above my heart."

Hope blinked in rapid succession before sighing heavily. "That is so romantic."

"Don't tell anyone." I dropped my shirt, "But I'm a closet romantic."

"Your secret is safe with me," she promised, as Ruby placed our meals in front of us.

We began to eat—me a fully loaded burger with a side stack of fries so high it threatened to cause an avalanche of potato if disrupted—and Hope with her stack of waffles, berries and peach ice cream.

I reached across the table to swipe a bite.

"Hey!" She blocked my fork with her own. "That's mine."

"We always share."

"Sure, before you became a big rockstar and started collecting all sorts of diseases from your fans."

I frowned. "Are you slut shaming?"

"What? No! I'm talking about colds and flus. Isn't that why you're here? Cause you had to cancel a leg of your tour because of a sore throat?"

I sat back in my chair, the delicious burger turning to ash in my mouth. "Not quite."

"No?"

I glanced away from her innocent curiosity, battling the emotions that threatened to overwhelm me.

"It's twenty years this year, and...." I swallowed. "The park is finally going to be donated to the town."

She reached across the table to squeeze my hand. "I understand."

"Do you?" I huffed out a bitter laugh. "Cause I don't."

"Grief isn't linear, Justice. We don't get to experience it and then we're done. It remains like a shadow over our shoulders. We can't remove it; we can only delay." She held my gaze, her deep blue eyes searching my own. "Don't deny what you feel."

"When did you get to be so wise?"

She grinned, letting go of my hand to pick up her fork. "I've always been this wise. You were too busy trying to kiss the Addler twins to notice."

I groaned, shaking my head. "What are those girls doing these days?"

"Women," Hope corrected. "And one is the pastor's wife and a stay-at-home mom with eight kids and loving it. The other became a stripper. Last I heard she was dancing out in Vegas and owns three properties and a fleet of cars."

I stared at Hope for a beat. "Is that a joke?"

She cocked an eyebrow. "I never joke about women's empowerment."

We resumed our breakfast, and I couldn't help but consider the differences in Hope. She'd always been funny, intelligent and too ridiculously nice for her own good. But now there was a depth to her that called to me—not that she hadn't always been a deep person. No, it was more an unknown element that made me want to dig deep and uncover all her secrets. She'd developed layers of maturity and experience that I had no knowledge of. But god knew I wanted to. I wanted to understand her, to work through the complexity to get to the heart of the woman who ate waffles like her life depended on it.

"Not to rush you," Hope said, glancing at her watch, "but I have a call this afternoon with a staff member, and I need some time to prepare for it. What did you want to talk about?"

I hesitated, knowing what I was about to ask would be pushing the boundary of our rekindled friendship.

"Faye's fielding calls about why I'm back in town," I said finally. "The media wants to interview my family about the park and Mom and Dad's accident. I'd like to keep the attention off them, if possible."

Hope frowned. "And what does that have to do with me?"

I cleared my throat. "Faye suggested that an easy way to keep the attention off them would be for me to be seen with a local girl. Someone who understands this isn't real and who won't get angry when we break it off. Someone without any secrets in their closet."

Hope nodded. "You want me to make some suggestions? I've only been back in town for a little while, but you could ask Nicole McCurdy. She's been hanging out with Bobby Fisher for the last few months. Or you could try Talullah. Though I heard she and Beau had a brief—"

"I meant you."

Hope blinked. "I'm sorry, what?"

I gestured at her. "You. As in, can you do it?"

Hope stared at me for a beat, and I caught a glimpse at something on her face that left me feeling off balance. But just as quickly as it was there, she shuttered it away, dipping her head to fork a giant bite of waffle. She chewed slowly; her gaze trained on her plate.

My leg jiggled as I allowed her time to process my request. It took everything I had to bite my tongue rather than press her for an answer.

"What about Roxy—"

"No," I interrupted. "It has to be you."

"But why?"

"Because I trust you."

She stared at me. "Oh."

I ran a hand through my hair. "Yeah. It's just...." I shrugged. "This life ain't easy. People will do whatever they can for their piece of fame and fortune. I've had women sell my underwear online. I've had men try to provoke me to fight them. I've seen the worst in people, Hope. And I don't have time for that right now. I just need someone I can rely on. Someone who understands the rules of this relationship and won't expect more than what it is."

She frowned, stirring her milkshake absently with her metal straw. "People will talk."

"I know."

She took a sip of her shake. "I'm not photogenic. I'll probably do something stupid or clumsy or say the wrong things or—"

I reached across the table to entwine our fingers. "Hey, look at me."

Her gaze met mine.

"There's no pressure here. If you can, great. If not, no problem. But let me be clear. No one, and I mean *no one*, Hope, is gonna fuck with you. I'll take the blame when this is over—I'll orchestrate some kind of bullshit maneuver that allows you to move on without any issues. But let me be clear, yeah, your face will be on magazines and they'll try to find some dirt to throw at you. But I'm not gonna let that happen. I'd never let you be hurt, babe. You're too important to me."

She swallowed, her gaze searching my face. "You're absolutely sure?"

"Positive," I confirmed.

We were quiet for a beat as she considered my request. My thumb traced gently over the curve of her palm, memorizing her soft skin.

She blew out a sigh. "Alright. I guess I could pretend for a while. But what does that look like? I have a job and a busy schedule outside of work, and—"

"Don't worry," I rushed to reassure her. "I can take care of everything and work around you. We just need to be seen out on a couple of dates. Maybe holding hands once or twice. That's all."

Her straw stilled. "Are you saying we need to kiss?"

The thought hadn't even occurred to me—or, more precisely, it had but I'd discarded it out of hand.

I wanted to know if she tasted like peaches, apple or spice. I needed to know how she'd respond, how her body would feel pressed against mine, how she'd sound when I backed her into a wall, cupped her cheek and made love to her mouth.

I decided to press my luck.

"Yeah, sweetheart," I said gently. "We should kiss—at least a few times."

She nodded, glancing away.

"Or we could just look cozy, if that's what you prefer. You know, holding hands, hugging, that kind of thing."

"Right," she murmured. "That kind of thing."

I withdrew my hand, waiting for her to consider my proposal.

"If I do this, will you do something for me?" she asked hesitantly,

"Absolutely," I said, eager to pay her back for the sacrifice she was about to make for me. "Whatever you need."

"Will you come to the rodeo with me? They're having a swing class and I've always wanted to learn but never had a partner to take and—" She broke off, shaking her head.

"I'm sorry. That's asking too much, never mind. I—"

Surprised and delighted by her innocent request, I couldn't help but reach back across the table to snag her hand, holding her in place.

"I'd love to," I said, sincerely. "It'd be my pleasure."

Her cheeks flushed, and I began to wonder if there was anything that didn't make her blush.

"Thank you. That means a lot."

I tipped her a teasing grin. "Though, not to brag, but I am pretty wealthy. You really could have asked for more."

"Like what?"

I shrugged. "I don't know, what do you want? A jet plane? A trip to Paris? A pony?"

She chuckled, the tension easing between us. "I'm happy with a night out dancing. But I'll keep it in mind."

I leaned back, rubbing at a strange warm ache that had rooted in my chest.

"There's just one last thing you should probably know," Hope said, hesitantly. "It's about not having secrets. There's this one thing, it's not a big deal or anything but—"

"Oh my god! It's Justice Wild!" The scream pierced the quiet chatter of the diner's patrons. Within a heartbeat a small group of teens surrounded our booth, thrusting notepads, pens and napkins at me to sign.

I shot a wry grin at Hope, who offered me a smile that said she was okay with the interruption.

I chatted with the teens, signing everything and anything and taking a million pictures. Finally, I glanced around and spotted my security detail, giving them the nod to intervene and usher them along.

On private land, I didn't need them to be so close, but out here in public, they were indispensable. The guys were staying in the local motel and running shifts to ensure that no one trespassed on my family's land. I'd feel bad if I didn't know exactly how much they charged me for their service.

Hope stood as the teens moved on, collecting her things.

"I need to get going," she said with an apologetic smile. "I have that meeting to prepare for."

Strain touched her smile, turning it brittle.

I frowned. "Is it a bad meeting?"

"It's... it's fine. I'm just having some issues with a staff member. It's not a big deal."

I didn't for one second believe her.

"Let me walk you out."

I scooped up her tote, tossing it over my shoulder before clasping her hand in mine. She glanced down at our joined fingers, seemingly surprised by my touch.

"Now seems as good as any time," I said, hesitating. "Unless you've decided to—"

"No! No. Now works." She squeezed my hand. "Let's do this."

It'd been a long time since I'd found pleasure in anything as simple as holding someone's hand, but feeling her palm press against mine felt right. Like a piece of a puzzle that I hadn't known was missing had finally been found.

You're a fool if you think this is going beyond a fake relationship.

Our hands clasped together, we walked out of the dim diner and into the bright lights of flashing cameras.

"Justice! This way!"

"Justice! Who is that on your arm?"

"Mr. Wild! Over here!"

"Justice! Why are you in town?"

I wrapped an arm around Hope as Mike and Wyatt cleared a path, Parul tailing us.

"Ignore them," I said to Hope as we ran the gauntlet. "And look above or below the cameras or the flashes will blind you."

She tucked herself into my side, keeping her head low.

I loaded her into her car, hanging on to her

hand for a brief second as the cameras continued to flash around us.

"You okay?" I asked, cupping her cheek. I found myself unable to keep from touching her. It crossed my mind to call a halt to this charade, to break the inevitable descent into madness that would launch itself at us thanks to the photographers behind us.

She smiled. "I'm okay, Justice. You don't need to worry about me."

But I did, and I'd continue to until this farce was over. I wanted to protect Hope, but she had agreed to this, and it would be over in a few short weeks. I just needed to keep the focus on me until then.

"Okay." I leaned in, catching her lips for a sweet, slow kiss. My eyes closed as the cameras flashed and people shouted questions. She tasted of peach ice cream and sunshine. Her scent tickled my nose, soft and sweet and surprising—coconut and lime.

It should have felt awkward with all these cameras, but from the moment our lips touched, the world around us ceased to be—all my attention narrowed down to her.

I pulled back slowly, reluctant to let Hope go.

Her gaze met mine, asking questions I had no way of answering.

"Thanks for the date."

Her lips tipped up in a wry smile. "Our first. And I didn't even know it."

"Regrets?" I asked, half joking.

She tilted her head to one side. "Only that I didn't ask for the pony."

I barked out a laugh. "Minx." I stepped back, shutting her door. "Drive safe."

As her car pulled away, I turned to the paparazzi, forcing a cocky grin.

"Now," I said, spreading my arms wide. "Who wants a picture of my good side?"

I spent an hour with the paparazzi, feeding their gossip reels and answering questions that allowed me to deflect their attention from Hope.

At least for now.

5

HOPE

Song: *Anti-Hero* by Taylor Swift (Cover by Dermot Kennedy)

*By "reacquainted" do you mean introduce him to
the delights of your peach?*

I parked in my space and sat in my car, staring absently at the house.

What the hell did I just agree to?

Somehow, I'd ended up in a relationship with Justice Wild.

Justice *freaking* Wild.

I traced my fingers over my lips, reliving that slow, sensual kiss.

He still didn't know I had a crush on him—

that much was abundantly clear. He'd have never asked me to do something so intimate as hold this space with him if he knew.

But damn if that didn't make it somehow worse. I felt like a thief, stealing time and memories that were never meant to be mine.

But what's the harm? He'll never know, and you'll have memories to last you long after he's gone.

I felt shaky and sweaty, my pulse uneven.

I should tell him. I should just walk over and tell him that I can't do this. He doesn't need to know why.

My breath hitched, my chest tight at the idea of abandoning Justice when he needed help.

My phone buzzed then buzzed again. I ignored it, but the buzzing continued, coming faster and faster.

With a sigh, I shook off my heavy thoughts and reached for my phone only to see that there were over three hundred notifications and counting.

"What the...."

A quick scroll showed that news of our lunch broke about five minutes after we'd walked through the paparazzi and Justice had helped me into my car. By the time I'd driven the short eight-minute drive home, the tabloids had already begun publishing images of us online.

I leapt from the car, sprinting up the porch to throw open the door to the house. Sure enough, Gran, bless her soul, was on the phone happily regaling someone with stories about me, my childhood, and the infamous Justice Wild.

"Gran!" I hissed, dancing from foot to foot. "Hang up the phone!"

"But it's Samantha. You remember her, Gladys' granddaughter. She works at the newspaper. She wants to know about—"

"Gran!"

She sighed, clicking her tongue disapprovingly. "Samantha, I'll have to call you back. Hope needs me. Yes, I'll be sure to call you back soon. You say hello to Roger for me. Mmhmm, and don't forget to tell Gladys to bring that jam recipe to the knitting circle. Okay, hun. You too."

She replaced the phone on the receiver and glared at me.

"What is so important it couldn't wait?"

The phone began to ring, and Gran automatically moved to pick it up. I thrust myself in front of her, physically blocking her from the devil line.

"Gran, listen to me. There were paparazzi at the diner today. Your number is listed and they're going to begin calling. Now, here's the thing, Justice and I—"

Her ancient answering machine clicked on.

"Ms. Higgins, this is Rob from TMZ. I'm calling to ask about the relationship between your granddaughter Hope and Justice Wild. If you could give me a call back on—"

I yanked the power cord from the wall, cutting off the reporter.

Gran crossed her arms over her chest, arching one salty brow.

"I—that is—"

"Hope Maree Hannah Joanna Higgins," she drawled. "Are you dating that Wild boy?"

"We're just hanging out," I hedged, unwilling to outright lie.

"Ain't no 'just' about it," she said, shaking her head. "This is a yes or no question, baby."

I winced knowing I'd have to lie to keep up the charade. My grandmother, god bless her, couldn't keep a secret to save the country.

"I mean, we've only had lunch today, but he said—"

"Praise the Lord!" Gran clapped her hands. "It's about time that boy woke up and realized what was in front of him the whole time."

I blinked. "What?"

Gran chuckled, patting me on the arm. "He's been hung up on you since he was sixteen.

You're a gorgeous girl, Hope. And it's a crying shame life conspired to keep you two apart these many years."

My mouth opened and closed like a fish, words failing me. Gran had to be wrong. There wasn't any universe in which I lived where Justice had liked me like that.

"I'll keep the phone off the hook for the moment, and keep my mouth shut about you and that Wild boy. But they're going to hunt you, baby. So be ready for whatever secrets they may uncover."

She glanced at the clock. "Don't you have a meeting now?"

I caught sight of the time. "Shit!" I scrambled to grab my laptop and rushed upstairs. "Don't answer the door!" I shouted over my shoulder. "Or if you do, don't say anything!"

"Don't you worry, honey. I've managed more prickly situations than a few men with cameras."

An hour later I clicked the little button that ended the meeting and tossed off my headset, fighting tears.

Ciara had finally decided to lodge a formal complaint against me. My boss called it bullshit, but human resources was required to investigate and consider the veracity of the claim. I was stood down on leave with pay until the investigation was concluded.

"About two weeks," the woman from HR had said. "This will be treated with the utmost confidentiality and privacy. I understand this might be a shock, and counseling is available to you."

I didn't want counseling. I wanted to do my job and not have my integrity questioned. Actually, no.

What I really wanted to do was quit my job and write full-time. But that would remain a dream for at least another two years while I squirreled my earnings away in hopes I could afford a salary one day.

I pinched the bridge of my nose, attempting to stem the tears that stung my eyes.

"You're okay," I whispered. "This is about her, not you. You've done everything right. You have the paper trail and the meeting logs. You're okay, Hope. You're okay."

The reassurance didn't settle the uncomfortable lump that had taken up residence in my gut or settle the anxiety-inducing small voice that whispered in my ear that I was a failure, a horrible person, and that maybe, just maybe, Ciara was correct in her assertions against me.

I sent a few emails advising clients I was taking

some unexpected leave, filed a handover note with my boss, and wrapped up an urgent project before turning on my out of office and logging off.

The next two weeks opened up before me like a yearning hole of despair.

"I guess I could write."

But writing required concentration, and with this cloud of uncertainty and angst hanging over my head, my concentration was shot to pieces.

Besides, reality seemed stranger than fiction right now.

I picked up my cell but hesitated to text Faye and admit the depth of my issues. I wasn't ashamed of my actions, but I did feel shame over how this had come about and how much it was affecting me.

Giving into a wild impulse, I texted her.

HOPE

Do you have Justice's number?

FAYE

That depends. Is this a friendly call to an old friend who is back in town or to follow up with him about THE REASON MY PHONE IS BLOWING UP!!!?????

I winced.

HOPE

Sorry about that. It was just lunch.

FAYE

I'd say it's more than that. Have you seen the picture? He KISSED you and is LAUGHING! Also, he texted me to say you're DATING????? What the fuck, Hope?? Since when do you date men like Justice? Don't get me wrong, I love him dearly. But the man has issues.

HOPE

He seems lonely, and I have time to help him get reacquainted with the town.

FAYE

By "reacquainted" do you mean introduce him to the delights of your peach?

HOPE

We grow apples.

FAYE

I meant your ass, Hope. And this is reason number one why you two shouldn't be dating. The man has forgotten more about sex that most of us learn.

HOPE

A person's sexual history doesn't define who they are or the integrity of their relationships.

FAYE

True, I shouldn't slut shame. I'm just worried about you. He's not the kind of guy you would normally date.

HOPE

The kind of guys I normally date have all patted me on the head at the end of the date and rarely call unless it's to connect me with their mom's knitting circle.

FAYE

That's happened twice.

HOPE

Try four times. But that's not the point. The point is, maybe I need to do something different. Maybe I need something Justice can give me.

FAYE

You mean the D?

HOPE

Not quite...

FAYE

I'm booking flights to bumfuck nowhere right now.

HOPE

Peach Springs isn't nowhere.

FAYE

It is to me. But I'll note that the bumfuck was in reference to the sex I have planned with Sam.

HOPE

TMI...

FAYE

Done! We'll be there later this week.

HOPE

I don't need a keeper.

FAYE

I know. But I worry. And not just about you. Justice has issues, Hope. Ask him to be honest with you about them before you get in too deep.

HOPE

This isn't meant to be anything serious. We're just hanging out.

FAYE

Babe.... You don't do casual.

HOPE

I might.

FAYE

You were meant to foster that rabid cat for twenty-four hours. What happened?

HOPE

Doesn't count.

FAYE

You had him for 6 years! And the bastard scratched you every day!

HOPE

He'd been abused! The foster people said he couldn't be adopted and they'd have to put him down.

FAYE

YOU ARE ALLERGIC TO CATS!!!

HOPE

And that's why god created antihistamines.

FAYE

My point stands. You don't do casual. I trust you to know what's best for you, but please, protect your heart. I don't want to have to kill the guy who helps keep me in designer clothes.

HOPE

Love you.

FAYE

Love you too, bitch. Now tell me
about the meeting.

HOPE

This requires an in-person debrief
and alcohol.

My phone immediately rang.

"An Uber driver will be there in twenty minutes with wine. Now talk to me," Faye demanded.

I let out a long sigh and moved to flop onto my bed.

"I miss you."

"Miss you too. Now tell me what's happened."

And this is why we were best friends. Faye understood me like no one else. Three hours later, I hung up the phone, slightly tipsy but feeling lighter. A second later my phone beeped with a text message from Faye.

FAYE

Don't make me regret this. And
drink some water before bed, you
don't need the hangover.

A second text followed with Justice's number.

Well, hello.

I placed the wine bottle on my bedside table, and rolled onto my stomach, contemplating what I wanted to do with this new information.

Everyday Hope would send a nice text like, 'Hey! This is my number in case you need me.'

But I was tipsy Hope. And tipsy Hope had a bee in her bonnet about the status of my life.

My thumbs hovered over my screen as I contemplated my message.

Earlier I'd dismissed Gran's comments about Justice, but her words had been playing on a loop for the last few hours.

Even if he hadn't had a crush on me, he'd still been one of the nicest people in my life. In the past, he'd made me daisy crowns and picked me flowers, he'd shared his last bite of pie, or saved me from strangers wanting to pet my beaver.

Maybe he doesn't love me, but... what if there's something there?

Sucking in a breath, I typed out a message.

HOPE

What are you doing tonight?

I watched the three little dots appear.

JUSTICE

Who is this?

HOPE

It's Hope.

JUSTICE

How do I know this is actually
Hope?

I frowned.

HOPE

You used to sneak Harley in
through my bedroom window
after a wild night out.

JUSTICE

Anyone might know that. Try
again.

HOPE

When my dad died, you left
daisies on my bed after the
funeral.

JUSTICE

How do you know that was me?

HOPE

Are you denying it?

JUSTICE

No. Just interested to know how
you knew it was me.

HOPE

Only one boy has ever given me flowers.

JUSTICE

That can't be correct.

HOPE

Fine. Only one boy to whom I am not related.

JUSTICE

Well, that sucks. You deserve to have flowers every day.

I melted at his text, desperately wishing I could return with something just as smooth and flirty but knowing I'd fail—epically.

JUSTICE

And to answer your question, I am home lying on a bed in my childhood room reading one of your romance novels.

I sat bolt upright, staring at the screen.

"Oh crap," I muttered, my heart pounding against my rib cage. "Oh crap."

HOPE

I'm surprised you gave them a go.

JUSTICE

They're good. Funny and sexy.
But, babe. This is what you're
into?

He sent me a photo of the pages of one of
the books.

HOPE

I see you've found the sex
scenes.

JUSTICE

Scenes? Over half the book
is sex.

HOPE

It is not.

JUSTICE

Fine. Like 49%

I grinned.

HOPE

Maybe I like that about them.

The three little dots appeared then disappeared then appeared again before finally his
text slipped through.

JUSTICE

I'm going to regret asking this but
what in particular do you like?

My breath whooshed out of my chest, and I collapsed back on my bed to clutch my phone close to my heart. There were so many things I wanted to tell him about why I wrote so many nasty, filthy scenes. Why I wanted to write confident women and fiercely protective men. Why I needed every book to have a happily ever after.

HOPE

From a book perspective I love being lost in the story. From a romance perspective I want the happily ever after. I want the sweeping gestures and the trials that make them stronger.

I hesitated, wondering if I was brave enough to take the plunge.

What have you got to lose?

Summoning all my courage, I added a final line to my text and hit send.

HOPE

I also love the sexy scenes. They're the kind of situations I wish I could experience. I consider them research for my future partner.

I tossed away my phone and snatched a pillow, holding it over my head while I let out a scream.

Yep, it's official. I've regressed to my teenage years.

My phone beeped.

JUSTICE

Research?

HOPE

You wouldn't count them as inspiration?

JUSTICE

Babe, some of the acrobatics described in this book are physically impossible. That aside, they are making me hot under the collar.

I sucked in a breath, forcing my thumbs to send the text.

HOPE

How hot?

JUSTICE

What are you asking?

I forced myself to type out my response.

HOPE

I've used my vibrator more than once while reading.

JUSTICE

Jesus, Hope. You can't tell a man
this kind of thing and not expect
him to react to it.

HOPE

Maybe I want you to react to it...

I bit my lip, frustrated as hell with the time
it took for him to respond.

JUSTICE

What are you saying exactly?

HOPE

Do you find me attractive? No
judgment if not, I've just always
been curious about your type. I
have to assume it's more slutty
pussy than full beaver costume.

JUSTICE

Slutty pussy?

HOPE

The woman at the Halloween
party.

JUSTICE

You mean Jacie? I think she was
meant to be a mouse. And no,
she's not my type. And I'm not
hers either. Jacie is into women
and submissive men.

I blinked, my memories of the last time readjusting. The mouse girl wasn't his type.

JUSTICE

And for the record—you're
beautiful in a sexy librarian way.
And, I know I'm going to regret
saying this, but you're my type.

I blinked at my phone, reading and rereading his text as a million emotions ratcheted through my body. How the hell did one process that the guy you were fake dating had a type and that type is you?

HOPE

If that is true, why have you never
tried anything?

JUSTICE

You're the sister to one of my
oldest friends. Not to mention
being a friend yourself. And I
have too few friends in the world
to screw with you—figurative or
literally.

HOPE

But what if I want to? Screw I
mean.

There was a long pause following my text

and I began to panic that I'd pushed him too far.

JUSTICE

Fuck, Hope. I can't say I'm not tempted. Being back here, seeing you... You make me want things I have no business wanting.

I tried not to swallow my tongue as I stared at his response.

HOPE

In that case, should we push this a little further?

JUSTICE

What did you have in mind?

I shifted on my bed, pressing my thighs together as a deep ache started in my belly.

HOPE

We could try sexting.

JUSTICE

I could do that. And what else?

I paused, shocked he hadn't brushed me off.

HOPE

Kissing.

JUSTICE

Just kissing?

My fingers hovered over the screen of my phone, my boldness rapidly deserting me.

HOPE

If I admit to wanting more, would you judge me?

JUSTICE

Depends on what you're after. If you said you wanted to spray-paint Mr. Cabot's barn, yes. If you're talking about me kissing my way down your body until I get to your breasts, no. If you're talking about me tugging your prim little skirt off and worshipping you with my mouth, then fuck no.

And just like that, my body burst into liquid flame.

HOPE

I didn't expect you to launch right in.

JUSTICE

Babe, that's barely foreplay. What kind of men have you been dating?

HOPE

None worth mentioning. Well, actually there was one worth mentioning but more in a "Ha! I can't believe how bad this date was" kind of way.

JUSTICE

So, we're no longer sexting?

HOPE

Oh! Please continue.

JUSTICE

Where are you right now?

I glanced around at the bubbled wallpaper and faded curtains of the ancient room.

HOPE

Can I pretend?

JUSTICE

This is your fantasy. You can have anything you want, gorgeous.

I closed my eyes, undone by his endearment.

HOPE

I'm in your bed and I want to be praised.

JUSTICE

Go on....

I hesitated.

HOPE

> Wait. Where are you in this fantasy?

He sent me a photo of him on the guest bed in Asher's house. The photo captured him lying on the bed, his shirt off and only the top of his grey sweatpants showing.

JUSTICE

> In my bed beside you.

Dear god, what was I doing sexting with a specimen this fine? I had no business even having his number.

But you do, a little voice whispered. *So why not see where this might lead?*

HOPE

> I like your tattoos.

JUSTICE

> Thanks, but I want to hear more about your praise kink.

HOPE

> Is it a kink?

JUSTICE

> Depends on how you react to being called a good girl.

Just seeing the words typed out had me reaching for my vibrator.

I may live with my grandmother, but I was a healthy, vibrant woman who wrote sexy scenes for a living. My vibrators had their own lock box.

HOPE

I like it. A lot.

JUSTICE

How much? Show me.

I stared at his request, wondering if I had it in me to be bold and send him a picture.

Drawing on all my courage, I reached down to touch myself, groaning as my fingers danced through the wet heat between my thighs.

As if he knew what I was doing, a text popped up a beat later.

JUSTICE

That much, huh? Naughty girl.

Sucking in a breath, I withdrew my hand and quickly snapped a picture of the moisture glistening on my fingers. I hit send then dropped the phone to the bed, grabbing a pillow to smother another squeal.

"What am I doing?" I asked as my skin became one giant blush. "Seriously, Hope. That's not sexy that's—"

My phone chimed with a text.

Hesitating, I slowly reached for it, cringing and half-wondering if I should run off to Australia before speaking to Justice ever again.

JUSTICE

Fuck that's hot. You're such a good girl, Hope. You got a vibrator over there?

Desire flamed, burning my embarrassment to ash.

HOPE

Yes.

JUSTICE

Good. Grab it for me. I want a picture.

I did as instructed.

JUSTICE

A sweet little pink one, hey? Take off your clothes, pretty girl. I want you naked for this next part.

My hands began to unbutton my cardigan before I'd even decided to reach for my top.

Without pause, I began to strip until the cool night air was the only thing covering me.

HOPE

Go on.

JUSTICE

Good girl. Now turn that vibrator on. Place it at your collarbone and slowly, real slowly, Hope, move it down to your left breast.

I followed his directions, gasping as the vibe rolled over my nipple.

JUSTICE

How does that feel?

I struggled to hold the vibrator on my breast and text, but goddamn, I managed it.

HOPE

Like I wish you were here to see me.

JUSTICE

Fuck

JUSTICE

Don't tempt me.

I hesitated, dropping the vibrator to the mattress.

HOPE

What if I'm not joking?

Those three little dots appeared then disappeared then appeared again. I waited with bated breath for him to respond.

JUSTICE

This is a really bad fucking idea.

HOPE

Is it?

JUSTICE

Open your goddamned window.

I wrapped a blanket around me then ran to the window and tossed it open. Light caught my eye and I saw him standing at the end of my yard, shrouded in dark shadow.

The phone in my hand vibrated and I glanced down.

JUSTICE

I can see your gorgeous breasts
from here

I hesitated before responding.

HOPE

Have you been there the whole
time?

JUSTICE

No. I made a quick run across when you said you liked my tattoos.

HOPE

That's a bold assumption on your part.

JUSTICE

To be clear, I never expected an invitation. I just wanted to be close to you.

I melted like ice cream on a hot summer's day.

JUSTICE

You want to put on a show for me, baby?

HOPE

What about the photographers?

JUSTICE

Answer my question first.

I glanced up as I hit send on my response, watching him read my text. Even shrouded in shadows I could see the tension in the line of his body, the way his head dipped as he read my one-word response.

HOPE

Yes.

JUSTICE

Good girl. Now get on your bed
and close your eyes.

Dropping my phone on my desk, I did as
told, sucking in a breath as I heard him climb in
through my window.

With my eyes closed, my other senses were
heightened. I could hear the gentle scrape of his
clothes against my windowsill, his groan as he
looked me over, the ragged sound of his breath
as he moved closer, cursing.

"Fuck you're gorgeous. Spread your legs."

His desire felt like a caress upon my skin.

Sucking in a breath for courage, I spread my
legs.

"Good girl," Justice praised, his tone rough
and full of need. "Now grab that vibrator and
run it slowly down your body towards that
sweet clit."

I could hear him moving toward me, positioning himself at the foot of the bed. I imagined
his gaze on me, sliding down my body in the
same agonizingly pleasurable journey as the vibe.

A whimper slipped free, and I smothered it,
embarrassed by my reaction.

"Oh no, pretty girl, you let me hear you, baby."

I shuddered, groaning as the vibrator slid over my wet labia.

"Yes," Justice hissed. "You work that clit, sweetheart. You're so pink and wet, honey. Good girl. Good, *fucking*, girl."

His rough tone sent desire spiraling through my body, lighting my nerve endings on fire. I moaned, writhing on the bed.

"Justice," I begged, my voice barely recognizable. "Please."

"Please what, baby? You want me to describe what I'd do to you?"

I licked my lips and nodded.

"Say it."

"Yes," I whispered, then cleared my throat, raising my voice. "Yes, please."

Justice made a guttural sound of approval. "Tease your breasts, Hope. I want to see your gorgeous nipples erect and begging."

I followed his direction shuddering as my body burned with sensation.

"Watching you play with yourself is torture, baby. I want to lick my way up your thighs and replace that fucking vibe with my mouth. I'd taste your gorgeous cunt, Hope. I'd lick you until my mouth knows exactly how you taste when you cream on my goddamned face."

I bucked, my hips thrusting toward him.

This man was killing me.

"Turn the fucking vibrator off," he ordered hoarsely.

Whimpering, I hit the button and let it fall to the side of the bed.

"Fingers," he told me, his voice rough. "Use your fingers."

My hand drifted between my legs, hovering above my curls.

"Good girl. Now put on a show for me, baby. I want to hear how wet you are. I want you to tell me every filthy thing you want me to do to you. Every filthy, dirty fucking thing. Don't you dare hold back."

I spread myself open with one hand, circling my clit with my other, my body flushed and needy, as I worked myself closer to orgasm.

"I'm wet," I whispered, embarrassed but too turned on to stop. "My hands are yours. You're touching me, circling my clit, driving me wild."

"And what are you doing?"

My breath caught. "I'm tied up."

I heard Justice curse.

"Keep going."

My fingers slid easily through my slick arousal. "God this feels good, but...."

"But?" he prompted, his voice a low growl.

"I wish you were touching me. I wish...."

"You wish?"

I shuddered, my fingers beginning to increase the pressure and pace as I edged myself closer to climax.

"I wish you'd hold me down and force me to take your cock. I wish you'd—" I bit off with a cry, shuddering as the orgasm gripped me.

"Good girl," Justice barked. "Ride those fingers."

I arched, imagining that he was waiting to enter me, his body primed. I spread my legs wider, placing myself on full display as I finally shattered, my body clenching as I came in a glorious, sweaty, wet mess.

"Fuck, Hope."

My eyelids snapped open, and I found Justice's molten gaze on me. He stood at the foot of the bed, looming large and imposing above me.

Slowly, ever so slowly, he slid his hands over his torso, pushing his grey sweats down until his cock bounced free.

I watched in stunned silence as he wrapped one hand around his cock, stroking and pulling, and twisting the mushroomed head. The tip of his dick glistened, and I couldn't take my eyes off the erotic vision he presented.

"Like what you see?" he asked, his lips twisting into a half grin.

"Oh, yeah." I licked my lips as I slowly

dragged my gaze away from his cock. "But there's something missing."

He didn't slow his pace. "And that is?"

I met his gaze with a hot look of my own as I thrust my breasts out, cupping them in hopes he'd take what was offered. "Maybe you could fulfill a fantasy for me?"

His eyebrows rose in question.

"Come on my chest."

His curse whipped through the quiet of my room.

He dropped his hands to wrap them around my ankles and hauled me down the bed. I thrilled at the easy way he handled my body, loving how he moved me this way and that until I was seated on the edge of the bed and he could stand between my spread legs.

"Cup your breasts. Eyes on me."

Our gazes locked as I did as instructed.

"Next time I'm gonna fuck these pretty tits," he promised as he rubbed the tip of his cock across one nipple and over to the other. "But for now, play with yourself, baby. I wanna see how you like to be touched."

I did as instructed, stroking my breasts and plucking at my nipples, using my thumbs to drive myself wild.

My hips began to rock on the bed, and Justice, recognizing my need, shifted us until I was riding his leg. The pressure against my core felt incredible as I continued to tease my breasts.

Our gazes locked, and in his eyes I could see the wild—nearly *feral* desire he had for me.

For me.

His free hand lifted, and he traced my lower lip, gently applying pressure to get me to open. Without thinking I did so, sucking his finger into my mouth.

Justice cursed, his pace now choppy and frantic. I sucked his thumb harder and a stroke later he tipped over the edge, moving his dick across my breasts, collarbone and neck as pulses of his hot cum licked my skin.

Without missing a beat, he reached down between us, his fingers finding my clit.

"Kiss," he barked roughly. "Now."

My mouth found his, and I opened for him as he played my body like song. We were in perfect harmony, every move and breath geared towards bringing me to the same climax he'd just experienced.

And when it hit, my orgasm went far beyond any of my wildest dreams.

We collapsed on the bed, both of us breathing hard.

"Shit." He lifted his head from my shoulder. "Fuck, we shouldn't have done that."

I thrust my hand up to cover his mouth.

"Shh," I said, shaking my head. "I want to stay in the afterglow."

He caught my hand and drew it to his mouth.

"Fuck you smell good." His lips closed around my fingers, licking them clean of my cream. "And you taste fucking better."

His curses punctuated every word, and I loved it. I loved how he couldn't seem to stop himself from touching me—even if it was only the most cursory of touches.

"Will you make love to me?" I asked, pushing for what I wanted.

"No, baby." He let my hand go to gently brush hair away from my face. "I want to build us up to that."

I pouted. "But I'm enthusiastically consenting."

"Mm, but rushing isn't what I want for us." He bent down until our heads were nearly touching. "Don't worry, I'll take care of you."

Justice caught my lips in a kiss. It wasn't a soft peck or a gentle hello. This kiss went deep and hard and was filled with a hunger I only vaguely recognized.

He drew back to press kisses down my neck.

"That was our third kiss," I said, tilting my head to give him better access. "And I'm naked."

His dark chuckle teased the sensitive skin of my neck. "You certainly are."

He gently lowered me to the bed, dancing caresses across my skin and kisses across my lips, cheeks, and breasts.

It took me a minute to realize that he'd found a cloth somewhere and had begun to clean the cum from my body.

I made a slight murmured protest, but his gentle touch coupled with the lateness of the house began to lull me to sleep.

Justice pressed a kiss to my forehead. "Good night, baby. Dream of me."

And I did just that.

6

HOPE

Song: *Unholy* by Sam Smith and Kim Petras

*I'm going to spank your ass until my hand is
branded on your skin*

I'd successfully managed to avoid the man for all of three hours since I'd woken up emotionally wrung out and with memories of an orgasm that would keep me blushing for years.

I hesitated, unsure how to respond to a man

who had not only seen me naked and climaxing but had come all over my chest.

I understood that I shouldn't be ashamed of our actions—and that he'd been more than respectful by not taking advantage of the situation.

But I'd never been in this situation before, and I didn't know how to deal with it.

"Pass me that green yarn?" Ms. Abernathy asked, nodding at the ball on the table in front of me.

I slid it across to her and sighed as another text popped up on my screen.

JUSTICE

If you don't tell me right now, I'm going to spank your ass until my hand is branded on your skin.
Don't tempt me, Hope.

I ducked my head to avoid the blush that had now become semi-permanent around Justice.

HOPE

I'm at Gran's knitting club.

JUSTICE

Which is where, exactly?

HOPE

The church hall.

JUSTICE

Jesus Christ.

HOPE

He's not here right now, but I'm sure He'd make a home visit for a sinner like you.

I slipped my phone back into my pocket when he didn't respond and picked up my needles once more.

With no work, I'd found myself at a loose end today and rather than stay home and wallow in the uncertainty and frustration of the situation, I told Gran I'd taken the week off and would come with her.

I had immediate regret as I became the center of all the gossip.

Turns out gossip rags had nothing on the grapevine—or the memories—of the matrons in this town. They'd spent the last hour rehashing all the highlights from my youth—including but not limited to, the time I broke my arm trying to climb an apple tree, the time I lost a baby tooth and didn't tell anyone, which led to me crying in the grocery store about the tooth fairy hating me, and the time my brothers decided it would be perfectly acceptable to turn up to my dance recital with moose horns.

That'd been just before Dad had gotten sick. The dance lessons had stopped soon after.

A tingle started in the back of my neck, and I knew without even turning that Justice had entered the hall.

"Well, well, well," Gran drawled, her fingers pausing. "Look what the cat dragged in."

"Ladies," he greeted, his warm voice sending pleasant shivers up my spine. "How are you today?"

I kept my head down as he took the seat beside mine, flirting with the older women. They were putty in his charming hand within minutes.

But then, who wouldn't be? Today he'd dressed down, wearing beaten jeans so old they seemed to have molded to his body. His shirt was similarly inappropriate, the white fabric clinging to his skin as if it had been made for him.

And the bastard hadn't shaved, his scruff adding an even rougher edge to his already wild persona.

I will not blush, I will not blush, I will not—

"And how are you today, Ms. Higgins?" he asked, leaning into me.

I finally looked up from my massacre of a scarf. "Just fine. How are you?" I asked primly.

His gaze swept across my face, searching for

something. Whatever it was, he seemed to find it as a small grin tipped up one side of his mouth.

"Sleep well?"

I held his gaze. "Very. And you?"

"Mm." He brushed a stray hair away from my cheek, tucking it behind my ear. "Must have been all the exercise I performed before bed."

The bastard knew exactly what to say to ignite my desire. I squirmed in my seat, pressing my thighs together as he turned away from me to answer a question.

Pull it together, Hope! Your GRANDMOTHER is present.

I glanced around the hall and noted his security detail standing discreetly in the corners.

Had they been outside last night? God, how embarrassing.

"Hope?" Gran called from across the table.

"Yes?"

"Could you go make us up another pitcher of lemonade?"

I surged to my feet, appreciating the excuse to escape Justice's presence and collect myself.

"Of course." I tossed my ruin of a scarf on the table, knowing the women would silently be judging the knotted mess.

Don't worry, I also judged myself. Despite

my many skills, knitting had never been one I could master.

I began to hurry from the room only to be stopped by Gran's question to Justice.

"And young man, can you go help my granddaughter? She'll need someone to help carry the food."

"I can use a cart!" I protested.

"Nonsense. We have a fine young man here willing to assist." She glared at Justice. "Isn't that right?"

"Yes, ma'am," he responded with a straight face. "We'll be right back."

Gran waved at us dismissively. "Take your time. The quiche will need a few minutes in the oven to warm it up."

I spluttered as Justice placed a hand on the small of my back and gently guided me from the room.

Betrayed by my own flesh and blood. I couldn't believe it.

The kitchen sat on the far side of the building. The building had once been a barn before the family had gifted it to the church many a century ago.

I wasn't religious, and I didn't think my gran felt a particular commitment to the church so much as used it as an opportunity to commune with her fellow townsfolk.

But I respected the institution enough to recognize that Justice turning me on inside these hallowed walls would probably not be looked on fondly by the clergy.

Unfortunately, he didn't seem to hold the same views.

"You avoiding me?" he asked when I pulled away from him as we entered the kitchen.

"No, not at all," I lied sweetly. "I'm just busy with Gran today."

I twisted the knob on the oven then moved to the fridge to pull out Gran's quiche.

Justice watched me for a beat, his dark gaze unreadable. Then he shrugged, rolling his shoulders as if to discard whatever had settled on them.

"What can I do to help?"

I slid the quiche in the oven and twisted the ancient timer then pointed at the empty jugs in the middle of the kitchen counter. "You can start mixing the lemonade while I cut the sandwiches, if you'd like."

"Done."

We moved around the kitchen in a strangely silent dance, somehow in tune with one another despite the lack of verbal communication.

Justice finally broke the silence.

"You know you have nothing to be ashamed of, right?"

"I know." I kept my head bent, hiding my expression behind the curtain of my hair. "That doesn't mean I'm ready to look at you, though."

He pulled a chopping board free and set it down beside mine, twirling a knife in one hand as he reached for a sandwich with the other.

"Why not?" he asked, slicing into the soft bread.

"Because if I do, I'm pretty sure I'm going to do something stupid."

His knife stilled. "What kind of stupid?"

"Ask you to lay me out on the counter of the church kitchen and kiss me, stupid."

He remained quiet and still for a breath before leaning in to ask the question on his mind. "And that's a bad thing how?"

I gestured at our surrounds. The room hadn't been updated since the early 1970s, and it showed. Wood laminate cupboards were faded and peeling, while the chipped lime green countertops clashed wildly with the formerly pink and now some sort of cream-slash-off-grey walls.

'Not exactly the most romantic place in the world."

"Hey." Justice caught my chin, turning me until I faced him. "Ignore that. Being with you is what makes this romantic." He stepped into my space, shifting us until my butt hit the island counter, halting my retreat.

"Now, let me have a taste."

My eyelids fluttered, the pulse in my neck beating a million miles an hour as he leaned in, slowly, ever so slowly until his breath brushed my lips.

This isn't real.

Finally his lips took mine in a hungry, leisurely kiss.

For him this relationship had an expiry date. Whatever had occurred between us last night might have taken us over the edge, but in the light of the day I had regrets. There wasn't any way to put that experience back into the unknown box. Now that I knew how he tasted, how he sounded, how he looked, each moment with him felt easier and harder.

"Justice...." My protest died as he deepened our kiss.

"Good girl," he murmured. "Now stay here while I indulge."

His kiss tasted of sunshine and overturned regrets. Each drag of his lips built upon the last until I couldn't tell where one ended and another began.

My arms wrapped around his neck, and I tilted my head to grant him better access.

I wanted more.

More of this.

More of him.

More, more, more.

A small voice queried if he really wanted me or if I was simply convenient.

But I knew, deep down, that there was no turning back from this path we'd found ourselves on.

"Let's see," Justice murmured against my lips. "Sober." He kissed his way down my neck, nibbling at my collarbone as his hands fisted my skirt. "But are you enthusiastically consenting?"

In the cold light of day, it would be so easy to deny him. To request that he step back and stop.

But I didn't want him to.

Crap. I think I'm going to hell.

His hand slipped under my skirt and began to stroke across the damp fabric of my underwear.

"So wet, baby." He nipped my earlobe. "You been needing relief all day or just since I got here?"

"All day," I admitted. "I played with myself this morning."

"Fuck you're a naughty girl." His finger ran up and down my slit, the fabric adding a delicious friction I'd never anticipated.

"More," I panted, eyes firmly closed. "Please, Justice. More."

He chuckled, low and deep. "Patience, sweetheart. You'll take what I give you and enjoy it."

He withdrew his hand, and I made a sound of protest which gave way to a startled yelp as he hauled me into his arms and sat me on the edge of the countertop.

With a wicked grin, he dropped to his knees and disappeared under my skirt.

"Justice!"

His mouth closed over the cotton of my underwear, teasing, and circling, pressing and rubbing, edging me until I wanted to scream from need.

"Love those sounds you're making, baby girl. Keep it up."

I begged. I panted. I moaned. I wanted it to end. I wanted him to keep touching me forever.

Justice Wild had his mouth on me. All of my hopes and dreams and secret smutty desires paled in comparison to this moment.

"You ready for more?" he asked, hooking a finger into my underwear.

"Yes. Please, make me come."

"Fuck." He ripped my underwear from my body and tossed my skirts up to my waist. Hitching his shoulders under my knees, he moved me this way and that until I was spread across the counter like a dessert waiting to be devoured.

"Gonna enjoy this." His head dipped and with one swipe of his tongue I lost all sense of time and place.

"Justice!"

He didn't answer as his tongue slowly rolled over my most intimate places, caressing me with care and adoration.

"Why are you going so slow?" I asked, reaching down to fist his hair.

"You don't rush what deserves to be savored."

His fingers tangled in my damp curls, complementing his gentle kisses with blunt, rough caresses. The juxtaposition between the two had me arching, aching, panting for more.

I could feel his grin against me. "Enjoying that, hmm?"

"Maybe," I lied. "Keep going and I might be able to tell you."

His dark chuckle sent my heart into a flutter.

He resumed his leisurely exploration, seemingly in no rush to end my erotic torture.

"Hurry," I directed, arching my hips in a bold invitation. His teeth gently grazed my clit.

"Why does this feel so good?"

"Because I'm touching you. Because your

taste is on my tongue." He dipped his head to continue working me over, driving my need higher.

"Justice?"

"Mm?"

"Can I taste you?"

Justice lifted his head. "And what exactly do you mean by that?"

I met his gaze boldly. "I want to taste your cock."

With a groan, he buried his head between my thighs, returning to his previous attentions.

"Is that a no?" I asked, my eyes drifting closed.

"Be quiet and let me enjoy," he growled.

Well, okay.

He picked up the pace, using fingers and tongue to devastating effect. He owned me, marking me with his possessive touches.

My focus narrowed, my attention riveted to each movement.

Distantly, I registered a small beeping sound.

"What's—"

"Ignore it," Justice barked. "Focus on me."

I did as ordered, panting and gasping, desire slicking my thighs.

"More," I begged, squirming under his tongue. "More."

He layered his movements, building the delicious tension until he slipped first one then another finger into me, his thumb trading caresses of my clit with his tongue.

"Fuck," I gasped then squealed when he spanked my ass.

"Language," he admonished, chuckling. "You're in a church."

He drew back, standing to lean over me, his fingers unforgiving as he pushed me harder and higher.

"Gonna watch you come," he muttered, playing my body to perfection.

I fractured, shattering against his hand. He caught my scream with his mouth, kissing me through my climax and smothering the needy noises I couldn't restrain.

"Fuck," he muttered, leaning down to nip my neck. "You're fucking gorgeous." He sucked away the sharp sting. "One more. I need to hear you again."

He slid down my body and back to crouch between my legs. He pressed his mouth to me, beginning to build me back up, playing my body like the professional musician he was.

His tongue circled once, twice, while his finger pressed against my G-spot, stroking me inside and out.

Already oversensitized, I couldn't halt the

crash. I bowed off the counter as painful-sweet waves washed over me. Pleasure sizzled across my skin as I slowly registered that I was lying on a counter in a church hall, with my grand-mother and her knitting friends a mere half a building away.

"Balls," I whispered, blinking up at Justice. "Are we going to hell?"

He chuckled. "Not today."

A gloriously lethargic feeling invaded my limbs, at the same time I registered an incessant beeping noise.

"What's that?" I asked.

"The oven. Ignore it." Justice gently drew down the skirt of my dress. "You okay, gor-geous?" he asked.

"Mm," I murmured, luxuriating in the after-glow of my climax. "Just enjoying the moment."

I heard him moving around the kitchen, washing his hands and turning off the timer before he removed the quiche. A faint bitter smell tickled my nostrils.

"Damn." I pushed up onto my elbows. "Did we burn it?"

Justice lifted the hot glass dish above his head, squinting at the bottom. "Just a smidge. We'll blame it on the oven."

I could quite clearly see that his "smidge" did not adequately cover the reality of our transgression. The pastry had turned a crisp, charcoal black.

My gaze dropped to his crotch, and I was immensely gratified to see that despite his nonchalance, his body showed his arousal.

We returned to the gathering, and despite some gentle ribbing about taking our sweet time, no one commented on the quiche.

I suspected it had less to do with politeness and more to do with Justice's arm over my shoulder and his lips nuzzling against my temple. It appeared the gossip groupies would have something new to chew over tonight.

As the gathering wrapped up, Gran passed Justice my sacrificial scarf.

"This is what you're getting yourself into with my granddaughter," she told him solemnly.

Quick as a whip, Justice pulled his phone out of his back pocket and handed it to Gran. She examined the offering and began to chuckle.

"And this is what she's getting into with me."

Gran handed me the phone which showed him... well, I didn't even know how to describe what I was seeing.

"What *is* this?" I asked, mystified.

"When we were just starting to take off, the band got offered a gig in Japan. As part of the promotion, we were invited on a local game show. This is a still from that footage."

The whole band wore costumes of some kind—very elaborate, very strange costumes that seemed to consist of leopard print fur in various color patterns.

"There's footage, you say?" I asked, hiding my smile. "And where might I find—?"

He slapped a hand over my mouth, pulling me into him.

"Ssshhh, this is all a fever dream."

I licked his palm, laughing.

"Do that again," he said, leaning in to whisper in my ear. "But do it near my c—"

"Will you carry this?" Gran asked, thrusting her basket of yarn at Justice.

He let me go and accepted the basket, then offered Gran his arm. "May I escort you out?"

Gran tittered like a teenager, and I saw where I got my thin cheeks from as she blushed. "You may."

She took his arm, and they walked outside, discussing goodness only knew what.

After loading everything in the car, Justice helped me into the driver's seat, hovering at my open door.

"You need to shut it or get in," I said with a laugh.

"Will you help me with something?" he blurted, fidgeting from foot to foot.

I sobered. "If I can."

"I want to see... that is... I haven't been back to see...." He cleared his throat, but I didn't need him to explain—I already knew.

"I'll come with you to see your parents." I squeezed his hand, my heart hurting for him. "Text me and I'll be there."

He bent to kiss my forehead. "Thank you."

"Any time."

He shut the door and I pulled the car away from the curb, wishing I could linger in the church parking lot for just a few minutes more.

Gran made a sound in her throat, interrupting my musing. I glanced over and laughed at her smug expression.

"Don't look at me that way," I warned. "This has nothing to do with you and your match-making nonsense."

"Maybe not, but I like to take it as a sign of success that we forced everyone to eat burnt quiche."

Groaning, I drove us home.

7

JUSTICE

Songs:
Days like This by Van Morrison (Cover by
Dermot Kennedy)
Fast Car by Tracy Chapman

Her blush had become my favorite color

The weather felt far too jovial for such a somber occasion.

I sat in my truck drumming my fingers against the steering wheel while waiting for Hope to show.

I didn't know when exactly she'd become my person, but here we were. I'd been back in town all of a week, and each day had been spent with her.

Hope delighted and surprised me in equal measure. Tough, funny, smart and resilient, I'd always considered Hope to be off limits—even though she was the exact woman I normally went for. But removing the barriers—and god had she broken those down—made me want her more than I could ever imagine.

I'd slowed us down not because I didn't want her but because I wanted to savor every second of the buildup—the looking, the touching, the tasting, the being.

Somewhere in the last few days, the line had become blurred. I knew I needed to stop this before it went too far, but I couldn't.

And fuck if that didn't make me a fucking selfish bastard.

A family of sparrows flew through the cemetery, cruising through the grave markers to settle in the shadowed branches of a peach blossom.

When I'd last been here, the tree had been a sapling, weak and vulnerable. Now it towered over the gravestones, adding a tragic beauty to the field.

Hope's knuckles rapped against the window of my truck, jerking me from my morose thoughts.

"Ready?" she asked. She looked like a fucking Stepford wife with her big doe eyes, and her gorgeous dark hair curling gently down around her shoulders. She wore some kind of yellow sundress that was far too modest while simultaneously being the biggest cock-teasing dress I'd ever seen on a woman.

No, I wanted to say. *Let's go get drunk and fuck the memories away.*

My mouth watered for a taste of beer followed by a taste of her, but I ignored the impulse, gritting my teeth and forcing a nod.

I exited my truck and Hope handed me a basket.

"Here," she said. "Carry this. It'll make you feel useful and remove the need to figure out what to do with your hands."

We began to walk, following the worn dirt path.

"Am I that obvious?"

She shook her head. "No. I just know the feeling."

"Fuck." I stopped. "Your dad is buried here, right?"

She nodded, turning her face toward the far side of the lot. "Over there. Well, his headstone is. We couldn't afford a proper burial, so we went with cremation." Grief lingered in her sweet smile. "We spread his ashes in the orchard. Mum likes to say he had a hand in the next years' bumper crop."

I caught her hand and tugged gently, pulling her into me. "Thank you for sharing."

She wrapped her arms around my middle, holding tight. "Thank you for inviting me. You're not alone, Justice. Remember that."

I took comfort from her embrace.

Out of the corner of my eye I saw Mike moving around the back of the lot, securing the area.

It seemed even this private moment was doomed to be interrupted.

I sighed and slowly let Hope go. She caught my free hand, entwining our fingers.

"This way," she said, leading me between the old stone markers. "Let's go say hi to your parents."

Their markers stood at the rear of the lot near a grove of trees.

I hadn't been here since we'd buried them twenty years ago. At the time I'd been an angry teen furious at the world for taking the two people I loved most. It had taken months before the anger had faded and the grief had settled.

And in that time, I'd become a drunk asshole, pissing off my brothers and fucking around until the whole town had known exactly how wild I was.

My feet dragged as we neared their stones until I couldn't move an inch closer.

Hope stopped beside me, her hand squeezing mine reassuringly.

"I should have bought flowers," I muttered roughly. "Or... anything, really."

"Open the basket."

I glanced at her. "Are you serious?"

She grinned. "I assumed you might forget. Being here is enough of a mind screw without thinking about what to bring with you."

I let go of her hand to crouch and dig through the basket. Inside, I found a bouquet of lilies, a blanket, a small bottle of whiskey, and an assortment of drinks and food items.

"I thought you might like to have a picnic," she said gently. "But we don't have to if you don't feel up to it. I don't mean to pressure you, but I thought—"

"It's perfect." I closed my eyes, fighting for control. The stinging sensation gradually subsided, and I opened my eyes to see Hope watching me. Her eyes sparkled with unshed tears, mirroring the intensity of my emotions. The afternoon light hit her hair, setting it on fire, and for a second everything I knew about my life and her shifted.

Hope had become the beacon of light in my darkness, a gentle touch in a world of rough edges. Her unwavering support and belief in me were like a lifeline, pulling me out of the depths of despair.

She asks nothing of me but honesty.

I reached out and cupped her face in my hands, feeling the warmth of her skin beneath my fingertips. "Seriously, Hope. You're fucking perfect."

She brushed her fingers across my brow, gently pushing my hair away. A soft, bittersweet smile touched her lips. "Not even close but I appreciate the sentiment."

We spread the blanket out while I steadily avoided looking at the names carved in the solid granite.

Someone came regularly—probably Fletch—to clean the graves and lay fresh flowers.

Hope settled on the blanket, adjusting her skirts around her and kicking off her shoes.

"Ready?" she asked, handing me the flowers.

I swallowed heavily. "No."

She smiled a sad, understanding smile. "But you'll do it anyway."

"But I'll do it anyway," I agreed, sucking in a breath. "Give me a minute."

"Of course." She reached for her phone and pulled some wireless headphones from her pocket. "Take your time. I'll be here."

I moved to Mom's grave and crouched to clear away a few stray leaves.

"Hi Mom," I murmured, feeling like a fucking idiot. "Sorry it's taken me so long."

My throat closed, tears clogging it as I placed her flowers.

I scooped up the whiskey, glancing at Hope who had her back to me, her attention on her phone as she gave me privacy even as she offered support.

"Dad," I greeted, placing the whiskey bottle on his marker. "I know. I'm an ass. I'll cop to it."

I shook my head, unable to find the words to express the pain that radiated as fresh today as it had twenty years ago.

"I'm sorry," I muttered, placing a hand on each of their stones. "I should have been there. I should have..." I swallowed. "There's so much I regret. So much I wish I could have done differently."

Mom's headstone featured all the usual information, her name, date of birth and death, her meaning to us, but one of my brothers had organized for a single lily to be cut into the stone. While on Dad's it was a line from his favorite song by Van Morrison, *Days Like This.*

You'd always know he was in a good mood when he'd hummed that song, forcing Mom to dance with him barefoot in the kitchen.

They'd been so full of life and love. Life wasn't fucking fair.

I bowed my head, letting the calm breeze and warm sun wash over me.

It took a while but slowly, so fucking slowly I barely realized, the grief began to make way for peace.

"I miss you guys. So fucking much. I hope you'd be proud of me."

I kissed my fingertips and pressed them to my mom's stone. "I won't stay away so long this time. Promise."

I stood, dusting off my knees and turned to find Hope watching me. She smiled slowly, gently, and opened her arms wide inviting me to take comfort in her.

She's my sunshine after the pain.

The line hit me like a bolt, my fingers itching for a pen and paper.

I ignored the impulse and moved to her, allowing her to wrap me in a tight hug.

In her arms, I find my ease, the words whispered through my head with the murmur of a melody.

I gently drew back from her, forcing a grin. "Alright, what did you bring me?"

She pulled beer, soda, sandwiches and cookies from her basket. "Take your pick."

My mouth watered for a beer, but I reached for a soda.

"You mind putting them away?" I asked, nodding at the alcohol. "I'm five years sober, but feeling a bit tempted today."

She froze, her face dropping. "Oh my god, I'm so sorry! I should never have—"

I placed a hand on her knee, halting her tirade. "Don't. You couldn't possibly know. No one outside the band and a couple of friends do. It's not a big deal. I wasn't an alcoholic, but I'd started down that road. After waking up in a different country and not remembering the last three days, I made the decision to get sober and I've stood by it." I offered her a half-grin. "It's also better for my skin. Or so I'm told."

She huffed out a laugh that sounded more forced than genuine. "I'm still sorry."

"No biggie." I passed her the beers. "Now, what are you reading? More of these saucy books?"

Her blush had become my favorite color.

"Not here!" she hissed.

"No?" I rolled over onto my back, shuffling until my head was in her lap. "But this seems to be the best place for it. Add a little spice to an otherwise uncomfortable situation."

"You're incorrigible."

I chuckled. "Yeah, but you enjoy it."

She rolled her eyes but didn't deny it.

"Speaking of." I pulled my phone from my pocket and opened my notes app. "Let's see, so far I've recorded fifteen sex scenes in the first two books, five instances of which included anal—"

Hope's hand slapped across my mouth. "Justice!"

I grinned, and somehow this fucked up day got a fuck of a lot better. "Too far?"

She handed me a sandwich. "Eat."

"Trying to shut me up?"

"Yes."

She glanced around then leaned down to quickly kiss me. "I'm glad you came."

I reached up to cup the back of her neck, holding her in place. "So am I. Thank you."

Our eyes held, unsaid things passing between us.

An aching need took residence in my chest. This thing between us no longer felt fake. I knew it was, but that didn't stop me from wanting more than I had any right to ask of her.

Slowly, I allowed her to sit back up and reach for her own sandwich.

"Now," she said, clearing her throat. "I'm unashamedly about to pump you for information about your tour."

I chuckled. "Baby, you can pump me for anything you want."

"Justice!"

Chuckling, I bit into my sandwich.

Hope hit play on her cell, Tracy Chapman's *Fast Car* playing through the speakers.

"You remembered," I said.

"Of course." She swayed to the melody. "How could I forget the first song you ever learned? You only played it every day."

With the song that changed my life playing, quietly we finished our lunch.

It was only later that night, as I lay staring up at the ceiling of my old bedroom, that I realized the heaviness I'd been carrying for years had dissipated.

Grinning, I rolled over and fell asleep dreaming of a woman in a yellow sundress.

8

HOPE

Song: *Say You Won't Let Go* by James Arthur

I feel like a high-price hooker, but not in a bad way

I tugged nervously at the skirt of my ridiculously inappropriate dress.

"Faye, this is a terrible idea."

My best friend tapped one finger against her cheek as she watched me from the other side of the computer screen.

"You're right. It is a terrible idea that I'm enabling you to fuck the man of your dreams. Take the gorgeous dress that makes you look like a high-paid escort off, and put that kindergarten teacher outfit back on. That woman looks like she's been in a sexless marriage for five years."

I'd asked my bestie for assistance in procuring a sexy dress for tonight's date. We'd express ordered five dresses, and while three of them were date appropriate, one made me look like an eighty-year-old spinster.

And then there was the final dress.

"Do you think he'll like it?" I asked, twirling a little.

"You're asking the wrong question. It's not about if the other person will or won't like something, it's about how it makes *you* feel."

I hated how right she was.

"I feel like a high-price hooker," I admitted. "But not in a bad way, if that makes sense? More like in a Julia Roberts, 'Big Mistake' way."

Faye nodded gravely. "All hail the original bad girl meets uptight guy romance."

I reached down to tug on my cowboy boots then examined myself in the mirror once again.

I'd gone all out for this date, treating myself to a fancy blowout at the Pink Peach, and spending hours perfecting my smoky, sexy makeup.

Not to mention the new dress. The little red number hugged my curves in all the right places.

I felt confident, sensual and ready to be ravished.

But brimming under the surface sat fear and a looming sense of the inevitable—this wasn't real. Eventually our pretend life would crumble, and I'd be forced to face reality.

I'd thought I'd known what I had signed up for—but each day Justice revealed more of his true self, tearing down the carefully constructed walls around my heart, making me feel things I had no business feeling.

I'd grown to know the flawed man that lived under the rockstar mask—and I found that I could easily love him.

No matter the outcome, I won't regret tonight.

I knew I'd have to let him go soon, but until that day came, I would embrace every second of this wild ride.

I struck a power pose, trying to draw on the feminine energy of the badass women who'd walked this earth before me.

"That's it, strut your stuff sexy lady!" Faye catcalled. "Woohoo! Yeah, you sexy bitch. Work that ass, honey!"

From out of nowhere she produced monopoly money and began to flick it rapidly at the screen.

"Faye!" I burst out laughing. "Where did you even get that?"

She shrugged. "Sam and I like to role play."

"I get to be the stripper!" he called from somewhere in the background.

"Quiet, you whore," she yelled back playfully.

Snorting, I blew her a kiss. "Love you. I'll let you know how it goes."

"Yes. All the details, please and thank you."

We hung up and I turned back to my reflection in the mirror.

"I can do this," I whispered, laying a hand over my churning stomach. "I am a sexy bitch worthy of good—no, great—sex."

I nodded once then spun, grabbing my bag and skipping down the stairs.

Gran sat at the kitchen table with three of her friends. They were, of course, playing poker.

"Gran!" I admonished, waving my hand to clear the cloud of cigar smoke. "We talked about this. No smoking."

"Psh," she grunted, flicking a chip into the center of the table. "We must have our vices and be allowed to indulge them."

"You go to church."

"To repent for said vices." She glanced up and then whistled. "Well, where has this pretty girl been hiding?"

I blushed, fiddling with the short skirt of the dress. "Is it too much? Should I change?"

"Depends," Gena, one of Gran's oldest friends said, eyeing me from behind her Coke-bottle-thick glasses. "Are you hunting for a man, cause that red will have them charging you like bulls."

I could feel the blush start at my toes and rush up my body, flushing my entire skin red.

I am a semi-redhead wearing a red dress and red lipstick. I'm the definition of a lobster.

I almost turned around to go change when a knock at the door halted me.

Torn between wanting to swap the dress and not make Justice wait, my mother's determination to make us the politest family in all of Peach Springs won.

"Come in," I said in a semi-panic. "I just need to change; can you wait a second while I—"

"Stop."

I froze, one hand on the door, blinking up at Justice as he took his time looking me over. His gaze slid from the tip of my head slowly down my face, my neck, my torso, my legs and back up.

He stepped into my space, capturing me around the waist and hauling me into him.

"Is the dress you're planning to change into going to show more or less skin?"

I swallowed, not understanding the glint in his green eyes. "Less."

He shook his head. "Sorry, darlin', but I'm not letting you go. This dress belongs on my bedroom floor."

God he was a smooth talker.

"Justice...."

Gran and her gaggle of geriatric gamblers chose that moment to intervene.

"And just what are your intentions, young man?" Gena asked, fiddling with her glasses.

"Nothing good, I can assure you," Carol said, flipping over a card. "Look at the way he's dressed! It's practically sinful."

I couldn't help but agree with Carol. Justice wore dark battered jeans with thick black boots and a white shirt that made him look as if he were gearing up to be in a photoshoot.

Over the shirt he'd thrown a blue and black plaid button up and had rolled the long sleeves up to his biceps.

I wonder if this look is the modern male equivalent of showing your ankles at a period ball.

The flex of his forearms did something to my insides, turning them warm and pleasantly tight.

"Ladies," he greeted. "I heard you had a game tonight."

He reached behind him and pulled a brown-paper wrapped bottle from his back pocket. Winking, he let me go to walk across the room and plonk the bottle in the middle of the game.

"Courtesy of your favorite next-door neighbor."

"Asher sent it over, did he?" Gran said cheekily.

Justice leaned down, kissing her wrinkled cheek. "You might deny it, but I know I'm your favorite."

She shoved him away. "Go on with you! Take care of my granddaughter. I don't want to hear her come home until after midnight."

He chuckled as I spluttered.

"I'll see what I can do."

She patted his arm. "And just so you know, my husband, rest his soul, soundproofed that attic room years ago. Was meant to be a games room before Alec and Lorrie moved in here." Her gaze turned milky. "This house was de-signed for children. Not death and sickness."

I opened my mouth, but Justice beat me to the punch.

"Alec had the best life and now look." He nodded at me. "Your granddaughter is back in the house. And you're going to outlive all of us, you old cat."

Gran chuckled. "Get out of here. Have fun!"

He grinned at the other ladies. "Have a good night."

Ruby lifted the paper-wrapped bottle. "Oh, we will."

With a hand to my back, Justice guided me outside and into his truck. The new veneer belied the age of the vehicle. It had been lovingly restored, and as such had older features like a bench seat.

"I'm sorry about that," I blurted as he pulled away from the house. "They're well-meaning if inappropriate."

He pulled out onto the main road then reached over and slid me across until my thigh pressed against his. Satisfied, he placed a hand on my upper thigh, resting it there as he drove us through town and out into the country.

"They're fine, babe. They care about you, and I respect that."

He changed the subject, asking about my day, making small talk.

"Did you find a house?" I asked.

"Yeah, but it's not ready until next month." He made a face. "I'll be bunking with Asher and the perpetual child for the foreseeable future."

I grinned. "Thank you for agreeing to come

with me. I'm excited to learn swing. It's been on my list for years."

"So this request has nothing to do with that scene in book three of the Savage series?"

"You're still reading them?"

He snorted. "Babe, I'm jerking my cock to them. This Stone chick might have stolen my likeness, but I'll allow it if she keeps writing sex scenes hotter than sin." He hit the indicator to turn us down the track toward the showgrounds. "Not to mention they're addictive as hell. Her writing is great."

The unexpected praise soothed a part of me I hadn't realized needed it.

"Do you really think that?"

"Fuck yeah. I even ordered the other series of hers—the werewolf one. You read that?"

I hesitated, wondering if I should answer. "Um, kind of. You see, I kind of am—"

My phone rang, interrupting my confession. Tugging it out of my pocket, I grimaced when I saw the name on the screen.

"Sorry, I have to take this."

"Go ahead."

I turned slightly away from him, answering the phone. "Hi, George."

"Hey, kiddo," my boss greeted. "How you holding up?"

I sighed. "I'm pushing through, trying to keep the anxiety at bay."

"Well, I got some good and bad news for you. You ready?"

I braced. "Tell me."

"Bad news, they haven't concluded the investigation yet. But the good news is they're planning to wrap it up by Thursday next week."

I huffed out a breath. "Okay, that's really good to know."

"Sorry it's not better news."

"No, that's okay. I guess I can't complain about an unexpected vacation—even if it's in such a horrid situation."

Justice pulled into the parking lot and quickly found a parking spot as I continued to chat with my boss about a few issues he needed to check with me.

"Okay, Hope. Have a great Friday. I'll check in with you next week."

We hung up and I sighed, staring at the blank screen for a beat.

Justice's warm hand wrapped around my neck, squeezing gently. "What's happened?"

I grimaced. "I don't want to ruin the mood."

"Babe, nothing could ruin the anticipation I have for seeing you naked."

I dipped my head. "In that case, I'm having issues with a staff member."

We exited the car as I explained the situation to him.

"I guess I can't complain about two weeks paid leave," I said, trying to lighten the mood.

He saw through my attempt at humor and reached for my hand, his touch grounding me in a way nothing else could. Turning me fully to him, he stepped into my space, wrapping arms around me in a tight hug.

Tears clogged my throat, and I clung to him, desperately needing his strength.

"This sucks. She's completely wrong and I want you to know that. You're going through a tough time, baby, don't apologize for needing to lean on me. How you feel matters. Your feelings, your struggles—they're not trivial. You're not alone in this, okay?" His voice was soft but carried a strength that enveloped me like a shield. "I'm here, sweetheart. You tell me you need to rant or rave or cry, I'll be there to listen."

I leaned against him, feeling the warmth of his chest against my face, the strength in his arms as they held me.

He's my safe space.

The bustling fair around us faded away, leaving just the two of us standing there—a world of our own making amidst the chaos.

"I appreciate you saying that," I replied,

feeling a weight lift off my shoulders. "It's been hard not to feel alone."

He squeezed me gently. "I care, Hope. And I'll always be here for you, no matter what."

I nodded.

With one final squeeze, he let me go but caught my hand, entwining our fingers.

"You know," he said, his tone teasing. "She sounds like a Fabergé egg."

I snorted. "I'm sorry, what?"

"You know, delicate and pointless."

"You're terrible," I giggled, appreciating his attempt to lighten the mood.

"I am," he agreed, pausing in front of an old-fashioned pellet gun sideshow stall. "Wanna shoot something to make you feel better?"

I chuckled, allowing him to draw me closer to the stall. "I'm a terrible shot."

"Good, so am I."

He handed the guy some cash then tossed me one of the guns. "Game on, Higgins."

Laughing, I took up a position as the stall attendant hit the button to release the tiny metal targets.

We shot wildly, hitting some and missing far more than we hit until our time ran out.

"Game set match to the lady," the attendant declared, handing me the tiniest prize in the world.

"What is it?" Justice asked, trying to peek at the item in my hand.

"Close your eyes."

He did as instructed and I reached up to slip the pin into the soft fabric collar of his button up.

"You can look."

He glanced down and laughed. "I think he might be on to something."

The small pin was a circle that read, "Last is best."

We continued to walk through the showgrounds, passing the bull riding and bronco bucking competitions and the roaring crowds. Justice guided me toward the food stands, buying whatever delicious smells tempted us; hot skewers of various marinated meats, slow-cooked candied nuts served warm, delicious green beans mixed with salty bacon and slow-roasted chili.

We traded stories as we wandered through the grounds, laughing about shared memories and learning new tales about each other's lives.

"Favorite thing about being famous," I asked, placing a Stetson on his head.

"The money."

I chuckled, discarding the hat for a slightly larger size. "And least favorite thing?"

"The money."

I laughed, straightening the brim. "I can see that." I stepped back, eyeing him.

"Okay, this is your hat."

He chuckled, dipping it in a nod to me. "Yes, ma'am."

Before he could pay, I had my card out handing it to the girl manning the stall.

"Hope, no. I can pay."

I placed a hand on his chest. "I know. But I want to give you something to remember me by."

The girl handed me back my card and I tucked it away but caught Justice watching me, his expression guarded.

"What?" I asked, reaching up to touch my face. "Is there something on me?"

"What makes you think I'll ever forget you?"

I shrugged. "You're a rockstar, Justice. Your life is big and bold and loud and exciting. This?" I waved a hand around. "It's hardly worth mentioning in your memoirs."

He caught my hand and tugged me out of the stall and across to a small, dark alley. I tried not to notice as his security followed, blocking access.

Justice backed me up until my back hit the rough wood of one of the pavilions. He stepped into my space, his green eyes on fire.

"Don't you ever say you're not worth a mention." He cradled my cheek, his thumb brushing my lips. "You're worth a sonnet, Hope. A song. A whole fucking album. You're worth the story that your life is writing. Days like these are what make life worth living. Being in front of screaming crowds is unlike anything you've ever experienced. It's next level. But that fades. This? These are the memories I hold close. Life is too fucking short to not spend it with people who bring you peace, contentment and laughter." He replaced his thumb with his lips, gently caressing mine.

"You taste like laughter and sunshine and home. And for that I'm grateful." He drew back. "We clear?"

I nodded, unable to speak around the hope that clogged my throat.

Maybe dreams come true.

He kissed my forehead then pulled away, catching my hand and tugging me into his side until he could wrap an arm around my shoulders, guiding us out of the alley.

"Now, where is this swing dance shindig?"

9

JUSTICE

Song: *Stand by Me* by Ben E. King

***You either let me drive you home or you're getting
fucked on the dance floor***

Swing dancing required concentration
and a connection with your partner. It
wasn't as structured as I expected, it was
all about feeling the movement together and
allowing for give and take.

It reminded me of sex, where every little
movement indicated where your partner
wanted you to shift and touch.

It took three songs before we found our

groove. For a guy who didn't dance that much, I had to admit this shit was fun.

Or perhaps it was fun because Hope loved it so much, laughing at every misstep and delighting in every successful spin and twirl.

"And now," the MC called, "one for our couples before we take a break."

The tone changed and the classic Ben E. King song *Stand by Me* began to play through the speakers.

Hope stepped into me, taking my hand. In unison we moved, our bodies pressing together, our feet in perfect step as I led her around the dance floor. Our gazes locked as the lyrics took on new meaning.

I slowly spun her out then drew her back in, her back to my front. With a small kiss to her shoulder, I kept her tucked there, holding her close as we swayed for a beat longer than required.

I spun her out again, and when she twirled into my arms, her head tilted up, ready for the kiss I grazed upon her lips before guiding her away from me once more.

And so it became a game, each twirl a challenge for my mouth to taste her skin, each movement leading to another chance.

I could have dismissed the significance of what was growing between us. I could have laughed it off and easily lightened the mood with a joke or intentional misstep.

But I wanted this for her. I wanted to give her this memory. I wanted to give her a taste of the beauty she gave me.

I pulled her into me, bringing her arms around my neck and gently gliding my own down her body to cup her hips. As the song wrapped, we swayed, our foreheads pressed together.

The couples around us broke apart, applauding the musicians, but I held her in place, determined to keep her in my arms.

"Thank you," she whispered. "Tonight has been incredible."

I slid my head down to nibble on her earlobe. "I'm telling you now, baby girl, you either let me drive you home right now or you're getting fucked on the dance floor."

She stiffened in surprise then tentatively pressed her hips against my abdomen, sucking in a swift breath at the feel of my arousal.

"Mm," I hummed against her ear. "See what you do to me, darlin'?"

"You don't think I need rose petals?" she asked, her voice unsteady.

I chuckled. "Baby, who says we can't match rose petals with hot and dirty? I've read your books; I know what you want."

"Justice..."

"Home or here, baby girl. Your choice."

"Home."

I grinned, knowing she'd cave easily.

"Good girl." I spun her out and then back, tucking her under my arm and against my side. "Let's go.

With my hand on her leg, I drove us home, teasing the sensitive skin of her thigh the entire ride.

The way she squirmed as I worked slow circles up and down her skin left me hot and wanting. My cock pressed against the zipper of my jeans, agonizingly hard.

I parked the car and moved, cupping her head to bring her mouth to mine, luxuriating in her kiss.

Her sighs and pants became my favorite symphony, and I committed each one to memory, savoring the trust she placed in me.

Her hands came to my jeans and fumbled with the button.

Chuckling, I rocked back, halting her. "Let's go inside before we do any of that," I said, mindful of my security detail that had followed us back to her place. They'd be discreet, but still, I didn't want an audience for this next part.

Quiet as mice on Christmas Eve, we snuck through the silent house and up to her room.

"Wait," Hope hesitated. "Do you have a condom?"

"Always." I pulled the packets from my back pocket. "I wouldn't risk your safety."

In response, she turned her back to me. "Unzip me?"

My mouth watered with the need to kiss all her gorgeous skin. "Come here."

I took my time pulling the small tab down her back, inching it down with excruciating patience. Each millimeter revealed another part of her that I needed to taste, to kiss, to caress.

Slipping off the dress, I turned her slowly then stepped away to admire her in the soft glow of the lamp beside her bed.

Her curves were abundant and perfectly formed. Each inch of her had been made for pleasure.

"Relax," I whispered, stroking a hand up her side as I guided her toward the bed. "The next bit will be fun."

She chuckled. "I'm not nervous, I'm anxious. I want this to be perfect."

"It already is." I followed her down onto the bed, laying my body over hers. "You already are."

My fingers tangled in the soft strands of her hair as I gently applied pressure, bringing her lips to meet mine.

I seduced her in fractions, starting with her mouth. The kisses started light and slow and gentle. But with each kiss I changed the angle, the length, the pressure until the kiss had no start or end.

With slow, deliberate movements I ran my hands over the curves of her body, gently removing her bra.

So much about Hope remained the same—her sass, her blue eyes, her romanticism. And yet so much had changed. Gone was the girl who'd watched me with sad eyes, and in her place lay a woman full of secrets and dark desires.

"Justice."

I moved down her body, licking and sucking, memorizing every tremor and tremble, each shudder and shake.

"Good girl," I murmured as I tongued her nipple. "Let me hear you."

Her hands flexed on my shoulders, but she stopped suppressing her moans, unleashing her tight control.

A near-maddening desperation began to grip me, my hands clumsy as I cupped her breasts, tasting the sweet salt of her skin, relishing her panting praise.

"That's so good," she whimpered, squirming

under my tongue. "I didn't know it could be this good."

I sucked, nipped and soothed, glorying in her unbridled reactions.

My hands glided down her body to hook in the band of her underwear. "Lift up."

Bracing herself against the bed, I easily slid the soaked material down her legs.

"So wet for me, darlin'," I drawled, fisting the scrap of cotton. "You're such a good girl."

She purred, stretching her arms over her head and spreading her legs without prompting.

God she's perfect.

My control shattered, desire setting my body alight. I tossed her underwear over my shoulder and slid my hands up her legs to grip her thighs as I leaned in, pausing only to commit this view to memory.

"Justice, please don't. I want to—oh fuck!"

My tongue swirled, licking at her labia, catching each drop of her desire. My hands trailed up her inner thighs, holding her in place, glorying in the rocking motion of her thighs and hips.

"Good girl," I murmured against her core, sliding one hand up to tease her clit. "You taste so good, baby."

Her breathy groan ricocheted straight to my dick, my head dipping to suck her clit.

"Justice!" Her gasp had me doubling down, determined to push her to the very edge.

Her hand snaked down to fist my hair, positioning my mouth where she wanted me, and I couldn't help but chuckle at her desperate enthusiasm.

In a blaze of heat, Hope came, her release flooding my face.

"Wow," she whispered, blinking up at the cracked ceiling. "I mean... wow."

"Mm," I agreed, standing to remove my jeans. "You ready for this now?"

Her gaze dropped to my cock, and she licked her lips. "Oh, yeah."

Chuckling, I reached down to fist my cock, giving her time to enjoy the view.

"You're gorgeous," she whispered. "It's not fair."

I shook my head. "No, baby. You're the gorgeous one. This?" I stroked my cock. "This tells you exactly how fucking gorgeous I find you."

"Oh, God," she breathed, one of her hands sliding down to cup her pussy. "I want you."

I raised an eyebrow, staring meaningfully at her hand. "I can see."

"Justice." She shook her head. "I don't know how to ask for what I want."

"Just ask. I'm here to serve, baby."

She swallowed. "I want to taste you."

Fuck.

I fisted my cock once more, squeezing my dick and stroking until a drop of precum pooled on the tip. Shifting closer to the bed, I leaned in, daring her to try and taste.

"Suck me, baby girl."

She crawled across the bed like a graceful cat until her mouth was positioned perfectly in line with my dick. Shifting until she could brace her hands on my thighs, I guided my cock to her lips, painting my precum over them.

"Fuck you're a hot piece, baby."

She purred, arching her breasts into my thighs.

"Play with me," I ordered. "This is your time to explore, darlin'. Be my wild girl."

She brushed my hand away, and took my cock gently, at first fisting me awkwardly before she worked out what felt good.

"Do you like anything in particular?" Hope asked, exploring the length of my dick.

I tangled my hands in her hair, my breathing rough as she began to stroke me. "Everything. Whatever the fuck you want to do, I'm gonna love."

She hesitated. "What if I get it wrong?"

"Avoid teeth and nails and we'll be fine to begin."

She nodded. "I'll try."

"And if we don't succeed, we'll just keep trying until we get it right."

Hope chuckled. "You're saying I need blow job lessons?"

I chuckled. "Pretty sure if you were to just breathe on my cock right now, I'd die a happy man."

She glanced up, grinning. "Guess we'll see then."

She started with light kisses along my length, then graduated to long strokes with her tongue before finally bringing me to her mouth and taking me in, one deliciously hot inch at a time.

"Fuck," I swore. "Fucking hell that's good. Keep going baby, take me. That's it, fuck my cock with your mouth."

Her eyelids fluttered and one of her hands dropped to between her legs to rub her clit.

Oh fuck no.

"Enough." I pulled back, sliding my cock from her mouth with a small pop.

"But," she whimpered, reaching for me. "I was just—"

"Trying to make me come when it's time for me to be buried inside you."

Her eyes widened, and her mouth fell open. "Now?"

I nodded.

She shuffled up the bed, settling in the middle to lie back and spread her legs for me.

Reaching for one of the condom packets, I tore it open with my teeth and withdrew the rubber, rolling it on.

Easing over her, I ran a gentle hand down her body.

"Ready?"

She nodded, and I couldn't help the filthy praise that spilled out of my mouth as I reached between us to build her back up.

My fingertips tangled in her damp curls before grazing her labia.

Hope panted, nipping at my lips. "Now, please. Stop teasing, I'm ready. I promise."

I chuckled darkly. "Are you just?"

I guided my cock along her labia. "You're sure?"

"Yes," she breathed, her hips shifting restlessly under me. "Please, Justice. Please, please, please."

Her begging broke my control. Dragging my cock down, I pressed myself against her, working myself into her with gently rocking motions, easing deeper and deeper.

"Fuck, you're tight," I swore, sweating with

the need to go slow when all I wanted to do was bed myself deep in her forever.

"Justice?"

"Yeah, baby?"

"Fuck me. Please."

With a groan, I did as she asked, thrusting hard.

She sucked in a breath, her body tightening in response.

"Fuck," I muttered, holding still. "Breathe, Hope. I got you, darlin'. Let it pass."

I shifted until I could slip a hand between us and began teasing her clit.

It took less time than I anticipated for her to begin shifting under me, her expression turning from pain to pleasure.

"Justice, please, move," she begged. "I need more."

I couldn't deny this woman anything. I murmured praises between thrusts, and I worshipped her glorious body, glorying in the gift of her trust.

Her hands clawed at my back, her demands growing louder and more desperate until I delivered her from her torment.

Her cunt clenched around my cock, her orgasm ripping away my control. A beat later I followed her, spilling myself into her body.

We collapsed on the bed in a muddle of

breathless gasps, tangled limbs and deliciously oversensitive skin.

We lay that way for a long time, my greedy hands unable to keep from running gently over her skin.

"Justice," she asked a little while later. "That was good, right?"

"Fuck yeah," I said, rolling us until we were face to face. "Best I've ever had."

She smiled. "So, you'd do it again?"

"You have to ask?" I kissed her shoulder.

"It's just… would now be too soon?"

I lifted my head, staring down at this incredible woman who'd somehow found her way into my life.

"Now, now?" I clarified.

She nodded.

With a barking laugh, I rolled until she lay on me, her body stretching across mine. "Give a man five minutes to recover then we'll see." I cupped her cheek. "In the meantime, kiss me. I need to taste your sweet mouth."

Hours later, as the sun began to touch the sky, I pulled the blankets around Hope's sleeping form, tucking her close against me.

Staring up at the cracked ceiling, I sent a prayer of thanks to whatever deity had thought to send me this incredible woman, then closed my eyes, ready for our next adventure to begin.

10

JUSTICE

Songs:
How Do I Say Goodbye? (Acoustic) by Dean
Lewis
A Lot More Free by Max McNown
Beautiful Things (Acoustic) by Benson Boone
Texas Hold 'Em by Beyoncé

Let's dance

S aturday night saw me doing something
I'd never done before—attend a barn
dance.

It turned out my girl liked to dance. And
fuck was she good at it. Her body moved like
liquid fire, lighting me up and igniting the tension that simmered between us.

I held her close, enjoying the fuck out of the feel of her body sliding against mine.

My dick particularly enjoyed the way her dress kept spinning up her thighs as she twirled, occasionally granting me a peek at her underwear.

The band came to an end with a flourish and Hope laughed, pulling away from me to applaud the performers.

I reluctantly let her go, feeling strangely bereft without her in my arms.

"We're going to take a break," the lead singer said, swiping his arm across his sweaty head. "But I've noticed someone in the crowd who, if you all cheer hard enough, might be persuaded to play a song or two."

I froze as the spotlight landed on me.

Fuck.

Hope's head tipped to the side as my name spread like wildfire through the crowd.

Double fuck.

I made a dismissive gesture at the singer. "This is your show, dude. I'm just here enjoying it with my girl."

But no one listened and soon someone had started up a chant.

I frowned, annoyed that they were interrupting my night with Hope.

"Sorry, we can go if you want."

She shook her head, giving me a little push. "I want to see you play. Go!"

My eyebrows rose. Many of the women I'd previously dated had been cool with my fame until this kind of attention had interrupted our time together. They hadn't understood that this came with the territory.

She pushed me again. "Go. I get you to myself every day. Give your fans something they'll remember."

I wanted to tell her how much her understanding meant to me, but the words were lost in the chanting of the crowd. Instead, I gave in to impulse, pulling her into me for a passionate kiss.

The crowd went wild as I bent Hope over my arm, dipping her.

"So romantic!" a woman screamed behind us as I brought a laughing Hope back to a stand.

I left her in the crowd and headed for the stage, accepting an offered guitar. I kept my back to the audience as I began to strum the unfamiliar instrument slowly, getting a feel for its sound.

Like people, every instrument was unique. Each had their own peculiarities and flaws that made their sound unique.

I fingerpicked the strings, listening to the

chords while I contemplated which song called to me.

"Sing *Hold On!*" someone called from the audience.

"*Witching Hour!*" another yelled from the bar.

Shaking my head, I adjusted the microphone and settled on a wooden stool one of the stagehands had brought over.

"It's a bit rich for me to come up here and sing my own songs," I said with a laugh. "Indulge me while I do something a little different."

There were some boos and general grumbling, but they quieted as I began to pluck at the strings, turning the sounds into some semblance of a song.

I glanced up and found Hope's gaze on me. In her eyes I read a million thoughts—all of which centered on me and what I needed.

"Someone wise said to me recently that grief isn't linear."

Over Hope's head, movement caught my eye. And there, walking into the beaten venue were my brothers.

Well, if that ain't a sign I don't know what is.

Without meaning to, my fingers began to pick out the familiar chords of *How do I Say Goodbye* by Dean Lewis.

I glanced back at Hope and cleared my throat. "I'm home for the first time in... too long," I admitted with a rough chuckle. "And being home brings up memories and feelings I thought I'd long ago reconciled." I dipped my head, breaking eye contact. "This is for my parents."

I heard someone swear near the bar and had to assume it was one of my brothers as I began to play the soulful song.

I adjusted the lyrics slightly, interchanging "mother" with "brother", and "darling" with "Justice" but the song otherwise remained untouched, speaking to everything I'd felt from that night so long ago.

As I hit the first chorus, I realized I'd made a huge fucking mistake. My voice wavered; the grief as thick today as it had been twenty years ago.

Fuck.

Movement caught my eye, and I lifted my head to find Hope standing in front of the stage. She stared right at me, her arms wrapped around her middle.

"Eyes on me," she mouthed as I continued to play, drawing strength from her watery smile.

My world narrowed to her and the guitar in my hands.

As I neared the end of the song, I began to

transition into the next, *A Lot More Free* by Max McNown.

Hope nodded her head in time to my foot tap, the tears now running down her face. She became my focus, my reason for being. I vaguely registered that the bar had fallen silent, the only sound my voice and the resonance of the guitar. All my focus remained on Hope and the need to make her understand that while my grief had carved deep scars, I'd begun to make peace with myself and my brothers.

As I moved to the end of the song, I took a chance and transitioned into *Beautiful Things* by Benson Boone, trying to put into words how much Hope had come to mean to me.

I finished and paused, waiting for her to say something—heedless of the crowded bar patrons and the numerous phone cameras pointed our way.

Slowly she swiped at her cheeks then grinned. "Now play something cheerful," she whispered. "It's time for us to dance."

A grin stole across my face, lessening the grief that shrouded me. "Yes, ma'am."

I adjusted the guitar and glanced up, finding my brothers watching me from the bar.

"You heard the lady," I said to them. "Let's dance."

And with that, I began to play Beyoncé's *Texas Hold 'Em*.

Laughing, Hope accepted an offer from Owen, allowing him to spin her into a quick-paced two-step.

Over the heaving dance floor, I searched the crowd and found Asher leaning against the bar. Our gazes met and he slowly lifted his beer, tipping it my way.

Grinning, I nodded back at him, feeling some of the grief retreat.

When I stepped off the stage an hour later, I found Faye at the bar with a cold glass of water for me.

"When the fuck did you get here?" I asked, surprised to see her.

"I pulled into this town about five minutes before you decided to share your heart with the world through song." She handed me the glass.

I accepted it gratefully, chugging the water as the band took back over and began inviting requests from the crowd.

"Sam come with you?"

"Tomorrow. I'm here to surprise Hope." She stared at me as if she'd never seen me before.

"What?" I asked, not liking the look in her eyes.

"I thought this was casual." She gestured

toward Hope, who was chatting with my brothers near the stage.

"It is."

She cocked an eyebrow. "Do you know that?"

I frowned. "Men and women can be kissing friends, Faye."

She nodded. "Yep. I myself have indulged in many of these kinds of relationships. But does your heart know that's all this is?"

"What are you talking about?"

She sighed and patted me on the arm. "You'll figure it out. Just make sure you don't hurt her in the process, or I'll leak news so gross you'll never have a gig again."

I sucked in a breath between my teeth. "Evil."

She nodded. "Hope's one of the best people I know. Ask me to pick between her and you and you're not even on the list." She rose up to press a kiss to my cheek. "I love you like a brother, Justice. But she needs protecting and you don't."

I hated the idea of letting her go. But this was pretend—and as much as Hope enjoyed experimenting with me, I knew she and I weren't destined for the long term. She had too much goodness in her to hitch her wagon to a fuck-up like me.

"I understand," I bit out, hating that Faye had forced this conversation. I wanted to stay in the fantasy for as long as Hope let me.

"Do you?"

I nodded. "She's like a peach. Sweet and easily bruised. Don't get me wrong, she's strong as hell. But her heart is tender. I'm not about to hurt her."

Faye hummed under her breath but seemed satisfied to let it lie. "Come on. We need to save her before your brothers make an ass of your woman."

I glanced over my shoulder to see my brothers pushing Hope toward the stage.

"Don't worry, I got this."

I marched over and caught her up in my arms before they could move her toward the microphone.

"You want to sing?" I asked, unable to stop myself from nuzzling her neck.

"No." Her head tilted back, allowing me greater access to her neck. "I want to hear you sing again."

"I have a better idea," I gently caught her earlobe between my teeth, knowing it would drive her crazy and, sure enough, she shuddered in my arms.

"What's your idea?" she asked unsteadily.

"You, me, my truck bed, and a night under the stars."

"Really?"

"Just giving you a little taste of what you missed out on in high school. You even have a curfew."

Her giggle set my body on fire.

"Um, so Gran's actually sleeping at my uncle's in Ridgemont tonight...."

"Let's go."

She laughed, tugging at her hand to stop me from pulling her out of the bar. "What if we get caught—?"

I kissed her, swallowing her protest.

"Trust me," I whispered against her lips. "I'm a Wild. We won't be caught."

11

HOPE

Song: *Body like a Back Road* by Sam Hunt

...a chant, a mantra, a prayer

As the truck bumped along the dirt path through the peach orchard, a flutter of excitement shivered in my chest. The moon hung low in the sky, casting a silvery glow over the trees, and the scent of peach blossoms and early fruit wafted through the air, intoxicating and sweet.

Inside the truck, music played softly from the radio while Justice kept his hand on my thigh, circling tiny designs around my overly sensitive skin. Each teasing touch stoked my desire, building up my aching need.

Justice pulled the truck into a secluded spot at the rear of the orchard and cut the engine. The quiet descended, and the sounds of the night drifted through the windows of the cab—crickets and rustling leaves, the river bubbling over water worn stones, and the occasional call from a night bird.

"Give me a second," Justice whispered, brushing a kiss over my temple. He exited the truck, leaving the door open to allow the cool night air to brush against my over-sensitive skin.

I heard him moving around the bed of the truck before he returned to take my hand and help me down.

"I hope this is okay."

Justice had laid out a soft camp mattress with blankets and pillows, a mosquito net had been propped above it, protecting us from bugs.

"This is beautiful," I whispered. "I can't believe you planned this."

"Never underestimate a man with a truck."

I grinned as he helped me up and followed me onto the mattress. He pulled me close, settling us down as the breeze danced over our skin and the stars twinkled above us.

I snuggled into him, tracing random patterns across his chest.

"It's been a long time since I watched the stars."

I tilted my head back to look up at him. "Why?"

His lips quirked. "Some would say I'm too busy trying to be a star to care about those in the sky."

"I'm not interested in what 'some' would say. I want to know what you would say."

He cupped my cheek, capturing my lips in a tender kiss.

"That I was waiting for a woman to teach me how to slow down and appreciate the night sky once more."

I melted against him, my lips finding his again and again. Our kisses were slow at first, and achingly gentle. His hands began to stroke over my body, soothing and exciting in equal measure.

Together under the stars and fireflies we built our own little world filled with passion and heat, laughter and desire.

Desperation built between us until I begged, gasping my need between heady, filthy kisses.

"Slow," Justice murmured as I kicked off my underwear and reached for him. "We have all the time in the world."

I bit my lip to keep from admitting how long I'd needed this. How long I'd wanted him.

"Besides." He flicked his tongue over my nipple then blew a cool line of air over the sensitive skin. "I want to see exactly how far you'll go."

"What do you mean?" I asked, arching up to thrust my breast more fully in his face.

"You said those books are a good insight into what you like." He lifted his head, his gaze finding mine in the dark. "I want to see just how much you like what you read."

My confession fluttered on the tip of my tongue. I wanted to admit my sin to him, to tell him my dirty little secret about all the fantasies I'd turned into stories.

But the impulse died a quick death when his fingers stroked between my legs.

"Turn around."

He helped me onto all fours, my head facing the river while Justice settled behind me. For a beat I felt vulnerable and exposed until Justice's hands teased across my back and up to gather my hair in one fist.

He tugged gently, tilting my head back. "Count for me."

"Count?" I asked, arching my ass up toward him.

"Yes." He sounded rough and slightly on edge, but there remained a promise of pleasure in his tone that made my breath catch in my throat.

I tried to nod but his steady grip on my hair held me in place, the slight pain that came from the movement lending a dark edge to our play.

"One."

The fingers of his free hand traced softly down my spine, his feather-light touch sending shivers across my skin.

"Two."

I gasped as he leaned over me and gently licked my earlobe. His growl of pleasure included a hint of a warning when my voice faltered.

"Three."

His free hand slapped against my ass, the sound shocking and strangely erotic. I found myself sinking into the heat his palm had left on my skin, relishing the way he soothed my stinging ass.

"Four."

He moved me suddenly, deserting my body. I made to look behind me but one of his hands squeezed the back of my neck, holding me in place.

The night sounds wrapped around us as the cool breeze tickled my skin. I waited, straining to hear what he was doing, desperate to understand what he wanted.

"Five."

With a slow, powerful thrust that ripped a scream of pleasure from my lips, Justice entered me. He held me still, forcing me to yield to his vicious need as he thrust violently into my body.

I loved it. I loved that he'd taken every single fantasy I'd ever had and distilled it down to this moment. I wanted more. I needed more.

I needed him.

Begging and cursing, I tried to move, tried to force myself back and onto him, to meet his thrusts with some of my own.

He refused to allow me an inch, forcing me to take whatever he felt content to give.

"Please, please, please, please." The word became a chant, a mantra, a prayer.

Justice picked up his pace, his big body dwarfing mine as he guided me into madness. Need rode us hard until my orgasm crashed over me, exploding my world into a million different sensations, each deliciously balanced upon the tipping point of pleasure and pain.

Even as I came down, Justice didn't release me. Instead, he shifted, moving in front of me until all I could see was him and his cock.

"See all that pretty wet on me, baby?" he asked, gripping my chin as he traced his cock across my lips. "That's you, pretty girl. That's all you and your greedy fucking pussy."

Said body part clenched, a new ache igniting in my belly.

"Suck me clean, Hope. Lick your cream off me."

I groaned and opened my mouth to take him.

12

JUSTICE

Song: *Earned It* by The Weeknd

The girl next door

Hope's mouth wrapped around my cock, and it was as if time had stopped. The only thing that mattered was the feel of her warm, wet lips engulfing me.

Her tongue danced and flicked, sending shivers of pleasure coursing through my veins. I clutched her hair as she eagerly bobbed her head, her eyes locked onto mine, questioning and unsure.

I groaned, brushing hair away from her face.

"You're such a good girl, Hope. That's it, baby, you work my cock. You like how it feels down your throat, don't you?"

Her confidence grew as I praised her, becoming bolder as she learned the feel of me. She dragged her tongue over my length, playing with my crown before sliding my dick between her gorgeous lips.

Back and forth, she teased and taunted, advanced and retreated, and I allowed her free rein to explore.

This would be the first of many experiences, and I delighted in her erotically sensual curiosity.

Hope's fingers teased my balls, gently squeezing and pulling as she slowly started to take me deeper in her mouth.

"Slow," I grunted, desperately fighting for fucking control. "And not too far, baby. Not tonight."

She made a sound of denial but allowed me to control how she took me.

I wanted this to be good for her—no. I *needed* this to be good for her.

One of her fingers dipped to brush across my taint and I arched my back, lost in the sensation.

She whimpered around my cock, her eager mouth enthusiastically sucking at me as her hands and tongue moved in tandem, seemingly desperate to bring me to the edge of my control.

I fought against the pull, determined to hold out—to delay my satisfaction for just one more breath, one more beat, one more moment of this perfection.

Hope tipped her head back, her gaze meeting mine under the silver of the moon. That's all it took, I was lost.

I felt my release building; the need to come down her throat nearly overpowered me. Instead, I drew back, hauling her up and spreading her across the mattress until I could cover her with my body.

My hands found the juncture of her thighs and spread her, carrying me down to lick her soaking cunt.

She gasped and arched her back as my tongue found her clit, exploring every inch. I teased her with firm strokes, then plunged deep, only to pull away and repeat the motion. She moaned and reached down to grip my head, urging me on.

Her wetness coated my chin as I continued to pleasure her, desperate to bring her to another climax before I found my own release.

I changed my angle, shifting until she began to writhe beneath me, bucking as she ripped at my hair. I could feel her muscles clenching with each thrust of my tongue, building her closer and closer.

I slid a finger inside her, curling until I found the exact spot I knew would send her over. Her hips moved in a frenzy, her cries turning to a scream as she arched, coming over my hand in a wet, sexy mess.

I rose up, sliding my cock into her clenching pussy, causing us both to hiss with pleasure.

Cursing and praising in equal measure, I worked her, slowly losing grip on my own control.

"Please," she gasped, her nails raking across my back. "Justice, I—"

She came, her body shuddering and clenching as my willpower broke.

I lost all reason, giving over to the primal need to mark her, to breed her, to fuck her with everything I had in order to ensure she needed no man but me.

My cock slid through her silky depths and within a heartbeat I came, fucking her through both our climaxes.

We collapsed on the mattress, a sweaty, gasping mess of limbs.

I rolled until she was in my arms. I couldn't stop touching her.

The girl next door. Who would have thought?

Slowly we came back to ourselves, our breathing slowing, our blood cooling.

She snuggled into me, her gentle sigh brushing my chest.

"Okay?" I asked.

"Perfect." Hope tilted her head back to look up at me. "I should go though. It's getting late."

"Fuck that." I rolled until she was under me and I could peg her down. Nuzzling her collarbone, I pressed tiny kisses up her neck until I could catch her earlobe with my teeth. I nipped gently, then sucked the sting away.

"Stay," I whispered against the shell of her ear. "Stay with me."

She sighed again. "I shouldn't."

"But you should."

"Mm." She sounded noncommittal.

I pulled back, searching her face for a clue as to how she felt. "Was that too much? We don't have to do it like that. We can try other things."

"No. That's not—" She huffed out a laugh. "I just feel awkward."

"Awkward?" I frowned. "About what?"

I could feel the heat radiating from the blush on her skin.

"I tend to look like a mess in the morning."

I relaxed, a tension I couldn't quite identify leaving my body at her admission.

"You could wake up looking like a sheepdog who lost a war with a pair of scissors for all I care." I stroked a hand over her cheek. "The important thing is being here with you."

She bit her lip. "Justice, there's something I need to tell you."

I shook my head, dipping to kiss the worry from her lips. "Tomorrow," I murmured against her mouth. "Tonight is for us."

With only a little coaxing, my girl gave in.

The moon sat low on the horizon when I finally tucked her sleeping body against me.

Staring up at the night sky, I waited for the familiar gnawing in the pit of my belly to awaken. But as the clouds slowly moved across the sky, and Hope snored gently beside me, the feeling that had plagued me since I'd returned home never came.

Huffing out a laugh, I pulled her closer and dropped a kiss to her head.

"Not again," she murmured. "Tired."

Chuckling, I closed my eyes knowing I had found a little slice of peace.

13

HOPE

Song: *If The World Was Ending* by JP Saxe featuring Julia Michaels

You became my main character

Something kept buzzing beside my head.

I ignored it, snuggling into Justice's side and burrowing deeper into the mattress he'd laid on the back of his truck.

He'd been right, this was the perfect spot for a rendezvous.

The buzzing started again but this time from two different places.

With a sigh, I blinked awake and grinned up into Justice's sleepy face.

"Morning," I whispered. "How are you?"

"Mm." He pulled me closer, burying his head in my hair. "Better."

This dream-like moment, being here under the early morning light with our whole futures ahead of us, made me realize how important he had become to me.

I didn't want any secrets between us.

"Justice?"

"Mm?"

I bit my lip. "I have something I need to admit to you."

"Is it that you're open to anal? Cause I can—"

"There you are!" Faye's screech broke through my early morning post-coital bliss.

We jerked upright, both swinging to stare at her as she stomped through the trees toward us, Sam hot on her heels.

"Get up! We've got a big issue!" She waggled a finger at me. "Your secret's out, Hope. And it's bad. Really bad."

"Secret?" Justice asked.

"I'm so sorry," I whispered, finally registering that the buzzing sound was coming from my phone. "I should have told you."

"Told me what?"

I began to search for my clothes, frantically

pulling on whatever piece of clothing happened to be nearby as I babbled at him—unable to look at his face.

"At first, it was just a silly idea, a guilty pleasure. I wrote fanfiction about a life I wished I had but knew I never would. It started with vampires, then shifted to werewolves before landing on rockstars. Then they kind of took off, and the rockstar fanfic morphed into actual fiction, and then that became romance and before I knew it, I'd started publishing these steamy romances. And somehow, without me even realizing it, you became my main character."

I whipped around. "I'm H. Stone. I started writing about the one man in my life who made me feel something close to love—and that was you. All those things you did as a kid—the flowers, the care, the respect—it all manifested into my writing. And I'm not sorry or ashamed of writing books that allowed me to dream. I'm not ashamed of writing scenes so hot they turned me on, or giving my readers escapes from this fucked up world. I'm not and I won't apologize for it."

I raised my head, staring him down. I had one sock and a pair of underwear on, and I was very aware that I'd somehow made a shocking error while putting on my shirt which had resulted in a breast poking cheekily out of the collar.

But I didn't care. Because finally, *finally*, my secret was out.

"That's your secret?" he asked, staring at me. "You write sexy romances about a guy who looks like me?"

"And other attractive men. And sometimes women. And sometimes aliens. Rarely any mechanical items." I bit my lip, waiting for him to respond.

"Where does the Stone come from?"

"It's my mother's birth surname. She took my dad's when they married."

Justice nodded slowly. "And that's it? That's the big issue? No kidnapped puppies? No secretly gross hobby like collecting toenails of famous people?"

I shook my head.

Justice grinned. "I'm proud of you and your filthy imagination. You've written books, Hope. Books that inspire and delight and turn people on. Do you have any idea how fucking cool that is?"

Faye, who'd been standing by the truck not so impatiently, interrupted.

"It's not about your pen name — it's the

work thing." She thrust her phone at me. "Justice's moment with you last night went viral and that *bitch* sold you out."

The bottom dropped out of my world, as I took the offered phone, staring at the screen.

"Oh god."

The headline damned me before you ever read it.

Rockstar Justice Wild's Girlfriend Accused of Bullying Employee: A Scandal Unfolds

Rockstar Justice Wild, known for his electrifying performances and wild antics on and off stage, finds himself in the midst of a scandal once again. This time, the controversy surrounds his new girlfriend, Hope Higgins, who has been accused of bullying an employee.

The allegations against Justice Wild's girlfriend surfaced when the current employee at the virtual assistant company, OnTime, came forward with claims of workplace harassment and mistreatment. The employee, Ms. Ciara Connells, described a toxic work environment where they were subjected to verbal abuse and intimidation tactics.

In response to the accusations, a representative for Justice Wild released a statement saying, "Justice is aware of the situation and takes these allegations very seriously. He and Ms. Higgins await the findings of the independent review."

The scandal has sparked a debate among fans and critics alike, with many questioning the impact this controversy will have on Justice Wild's career and personal life. Some fans have expressed disappointment, while others have come to his defense, arguing that he should not be held responsible for the actions of his girlfriend.

This is not the first time Justice Wild has found himself embroiled in controversy. In the past, he has been known for his wild behavior, including public drunkenness and legal troubles. However, his music has always remained popular among his dedicated fan base, who continue to support him through thick and thin.

As the investigation into the allegations against Ms. Higgins unfolds, the future of their relationship remains uncertain. For now, we hope Justice continues to focus on his music, with a new album set to be released later this year. Only time will tell how this scandal will impact his career and personal life in the long run.

JUSTICE TOOK the phone from my limp hand and tossed it back to Faye.

I couldn't move, couldn't speak. A strange numbness began in my face, flowing down my chest and torso and to each finger and toe.

I couldn't feel. Couldn't hear. Couldn't think.

I could see Justice fixing my shirt and wrapping a blanket around my shoulders, and in some distant recess of my numb mind, I registered that he'd pulled on his jeans, but hadn't bothered with a shirt.

But I didn't feel a part of it. I didn't share in the interaction. My emotions had turned me to stone.

Don't think. Don't think. Don't think.

Seemingly satisfied with my state of dress, Justice pulled me into his arms, holding me tight.

"I'm sorry," he whispered. "So fucking sorry."

A fracture cracked my smooth façade of numbness.

"It's not your fault." I swallowed against the lump in my throat. "Ciara is the issue."

"No, baby." Justice pulled back, gently brushing the hair from my face. "I'm the problem."

More cracks splintered, and I began to tremble. "You leaked this?"

"Fuck no, but I'm the asshole who asked you to be seen with me. They wouldn't have come for you if not for me."

Faye made a sound behind us.

"Can we get Hope home before we assign blame? I want to minimize the opportunity for the paps as much as possible."

Within minutes Justice had me in his truck, squished between Faye and Sam and wearing the black cowboy hat I'd purchased him pulled low over my head.

"Vultures," Faye cursed as we drove through the gates of the Higgins Family Orchard. The TV crews and photographers had arrived, all of them there for me.

And all of them there because they knew about Ciara's accusations.

A sob caught in my throat as Justice gunned it up my driveway toward Gran's house.

I wanted my own bed—not this borrowed one in a house that didn't feel like mine. I wanted to be back in Capricorn Cove where it smelled of the sea and crisp forests. I wanted to hide under a rock for a million years. I wanted to turn back time and never accept this job.

And all of this came from one person.

Wasn't it ironic how one person could fundamentally change the course of your life?

My days off because of the investigation had granted me time with Justice I'd never otherwise have experienced.

But now that was coming back to bite me.

Faye pulled the hat off my head and hurried me inside.

"Quick," she ordered Sam. "Swap clothes with Justice."

Sam and Justice did as told while she pulled a large hoodie from my coat rack and wrapped herself in it.

"If I keep my head down and skin covered, we might just be able to pull this off."

"Pull what off?" I asked her.

"We're going to be your decoys, driving around town to give you guys some peace. It won't last forever, but we can try."

I huffed out a laugh. "Faye, I'm whiter than white. No one is going to believe a gorgeous black woman is me."

She turned mulish. "They'll see what they want to, mark my words."

Sam pressed a kiss to my head. "Hang in there, little red. If anyone can pull this off, it's Faye."

I watched them exit, Faye hunched over while Sam helped her into the truck and off they went.

It took a beat but from the front window I could see some of the paps take off, chasing the truck.

"She actually did it," I muttered, shaking my head. "Damn she's good."

"Hope, we need to talk."

I turned to see Justice standing at the door. His hands were tucked in his pockets, his expression guarded.

"I didn't do it," I said, automatically.

"Oh, sweetheart, I know." He pulled me into his chest, wrapping me in a tight hug. "You don't have a mean bone in your body."

I murmured something against his chest.

"What was that?"

"I said, I do when you're in me."

I'd expected him to laugh or at least smile, instead his expression grew colder, more distant.

"Hope, I'm sorry."

My heart seemed to slow at his tone, and somehow I knew what was coming.

"For what?" I whispered.

"I never should have asked you to become a part of this. This life isn't what I want for you. It's not what I want for anyone. They'll make accusations, pay people for dirt, and if they can't get that, they'll make up crap just to see how you react." He shook his head, his arms slowly loosening around me. "I'm sorry, baby. But the best way to make this stop is to stop with the charade."

My heart pierced.

"What do you mean, charade?" I asked, my voice a hoarse whisper.

"We're not real, Hope. And I can't keep asking you to pretend with me."

"Is that what we were doing last night?" I asked. "Pretending?"

He glanced away. "This isn't real."

"Isn't it?" I pressed a hand to his chest. "Sure feels like it is."

He paused, his head dipping as his hands flexed as if he were trying to stop them from reaching for something.

For me. Reach for me.

He met my gaze, his eyes filled with a storm of conflicting emotions. His hand reached up to cup my cheek, his touch laden with unspoken words. Gently, he kissed me, his lips moving against mine with a tenderness that spoke volumes.

He made love to me with a fierce hunger, brooking no room for thought or feelings, forcing me to shut out the outside world until we fell into an exhausted sleep.

I woke to the sun high in the sky, an empty bed and a single note.

I'm sorry.

My heart shattered.

"Damn you, Justice," I sobbed, wrapping my arms around my knees as I curled in on myself. "This isn't how our story is meant to end."

14

JUSTICE

Song: *Stick Season* by Noah Kahan

She worth a fight to you?

I found myself at the place where my world had begun to fall apart—the bar.

I ordered a beer to have something in my hand as I stared unseeingly at the overhead TVs.

I had to break up with Hope.

My fame had exposed her to ridicule and humiliation. There wasn't any question that the charges alleged against her were false—but that didn't matter. The world would tarnish her with this brush and turn against her.

I'd seen it happen before and I refused to allow the media, the public, people who had no fucking clue about who Hope was, tear apart a woman who made me want to be a better man. The kind of man she deserved. The kind of man my parents had hoped I would become.

I wasn't sure how long I'd been there before Beau slid onto the stool beside mine.

"Thought I'd find you here." He nodded at my beer. "You drinking again?"

I shoved the bottle his way. "No."

No matter how tempted I was, I wouldn't go back down that road.

My brother made a happy sound as he sucked back the drink.

We sat in silence for a beat, both of us watching the game—though if anyone asked, I'd never be able to tell them exactly what sport was being played. My mind remained five miles down the road in an attic bedroom with god-awful wallpaper and far too much fringe.

That room would forever be where I'd found and lost my heart.

No, love didn't happen this fast. It didn't explode into your life like a fucking shooting star only to burn out because you'd dragged your partner into the spotlight, subjecting her to criticism she did not fucking deserve.

Her smile's like peaches, sweet and divine...

My fingers itched for a pen to capture the

lyrics rolling through my head. Lyrics that reminded me of Hope.

I need her like the earth needs the rain...

"Fuck," I muttered, closing my eyes. Her presence lingered over every inch of this town.

"Yeah," Beau said, tipping his beer toward the TV. "They're doing terrible."

We resumed our silent observation.

"Well," Beau said when the game broke for half-time. "At least now you can find a proper girlfriend."

I stiffened. "Excuse me?"

"Ya know." He waved his hand around dismissively. "One of those sexy model types. They'd look good at the Grammys draped across your arm."

I gritted my teeth.

"I mean, you could have taken Hope, if she'd still have you. But she's just not gonna fit in, you know? She's too frumpy. Too plain. Too—"

My ass was off my seat and my fist planted in my brother's face before the thought had fully formed.

Beau, never one to back down from a fight, bounced back swinging.

White hot pain burst across my jaw as he clipped me under the chin. I stumbled backward into a bar stool, grunting as I shook off the stars dancing in my eyes.

"She worth a fight to you?" Beau barked, as I blocked another of his powerful swings.

"She's worth everything."

Distantly, I registered yelling from the other patrons and the bar staff, heard someone call for the police, but I didn't pause.

I wanted to hurt and be hurt on the outside as much as I was inside. I wanted to break down every fucking cell in my body until I was numb from the pain.

Beau swung again, but this time I was ready. I ducked under his arm and crashed into him, lifting him off his feet and taking him to the floor.

We rolled, crashing into tables and knocking over chairs as we fought for dominance, trading blow after blow.

"Admit. You're. In. Love," he grunted between punches.

"The fuck I am." I shoved him away, but he grabbed me, holding me tight.

We never should have enrolled him in wrestling.

He slapped the side of my head. "Hope deserves better than you."

"I fucking know!" I roared, bucking like a wild animal as hurt tore through me. The pain

I'd been fighting, the guilt, the hurt, the overwhelming anger—it unleashed.

Beau went flying as I stood and reached for a chair, hauling it up and smashing it down over a table.

"You stupid fucker."

I froze, ripped from the hurt by my brother's voice.

Slowly, I turned to find Colt, Owen and Fletch standing in the door to the bar, their arms crossed as they glared daggers my way.

"Fuck," I muttered, dropping the remains of the chair. "Fuck."

Colt walked across the bar, his stride deliberate and slow. I swallowed, dipping my head to await the inevitable dressing down.

His arm wrapped around my neck, and he yanked me into his chest, crushing me against him.

A breath shuddered out of me, rattling in the silence of the bar.

"Let it out," he murmured, holding me tight. "You didn't cause their deaths, Justice. It's time to let them go."

Somehow my brother had cut through the layers of bullshit to the heart of the issue.

"You should have seen her face, Colt. Love fucking hurts."

A wave of regret hit me, and I felt like I was

drowning in a sea of missed opportunities and shattered dreams. I'd been blind to Hope's unwavering love, too fucking consumed by my own demons to see or appreciate the precious gift she offered.

Herself.

Every laugh, every touch, played like a bittersweet melody. The warmth of her smile, the silk of her skin—all lost to my stubbornness and fear of vulnerability.

How could I have been such a fuckwit to the woman who held my heart in her hands?

Colt clapped me on the back and stepped away. "Of course it does. You hurt because you care, and she matters to you. If you didn't, I'd be worried."

I blew out a breath, running my hand over my bruised face. "What the fuck do I do now? She's hurting because of me."

Fletch shrugged. "Damage has already been done. You can't put it back in the box, Justice. You gotta work out how to take her pain and make it less."

I swallowed. "I don't know how."

Beau clapped a hand on my shoulder, grinning through the blood running down his face. "I might have an idea." He pulled his phone from his back pocket and gave it to me. "She's already told you."

I glanced down at the screen, chuckling when I saw her books on there. "You knew."

"It wasn't that hard to figure out." He took back his phone. "Go write her an ending that'll make her swoon."

I glanced around at the bar and grimaced. "Shit. I better—"

"Go." Owen shoved me toward the door. "We'll clean up and add it to your tab—with interest, of course."

I chuckled. "Thanks."

"Don't sweat it."

As I moved to leave, Fletch reached out, squeezing my shoulder. "You gonna come home more often after this?"

I nodded. "Promise."

And I swear he smiled.

15

HOPE

Song: Girl Next Door by Justice Wild

Stay with me

I'd cried more tears than any man deserved to have wasted on them. My face felt tight, swollen and flushed.

I wanted to purge Justice from my heart. I wanted to let go of the dream he'd helped me build, wanted to free myself of the ropes that bound me to him.

Instead, I found myself unable to function, weighed down by the memory of his pause.

That stupid pause.

I rolled over, punching my pillow with a violence I hadn't known I possessed.

If only he'd left after delivering that blow, but that stupid idiot had paused. And it was that which kept me from cutting all ties. It was that moment where he'd stared at me, watching me with those big soulful eyes that seemed to beg me to protest, to fight for him, to fight for us, that kept hope alive.

"Stupid," I muttered, punching my pillow once more. "So stupid."

I couldn't be the one who chased him. I couldn't be the glue keeping us together.

Justice knew my heart and he had to make the choice to believe and trust in me or walk away.

He needed to learn to trust himself.

To trust in us.

I closed my eyes and must have fallen asleep, for when I next opened them my room was bathed in the soft hues of the afternoon light.

I frowned and moved to roll over and return to unconscious bliss when I heard it—music.

The guitar chords whispered through my open window, caught on the gentle spring breeze.

I listened, wondering if Gran had turned the radio—but then a far too familiar voice began to sing. I bolted upright in bed, my heart pounding as the song made its way to me.

"She's the girl next door
Always on my mind
Lost touch for a while
Now we're realigning
Her smile's like peaches
Sweet and divine
In her eyes I see
Stars align."

My breath caught in my chest as I slowly slid from my bed and padded across the faded carpet to peek out my window. My hands flew to my lips as a sob slipped free. There he was, standing on Gran's lawn in his beaten black boots and faded jeans, wearing a black shirt and the cowboy hat I'd bought him at the rodeo.

Justice.

Surrounded by hundreds—no, thousands— of daisies. He stood in their center looking for all the world like a romance hero.

My hero.

His fingers picked at the chords as he sang lyrics that spoke directly to my heart.

"We were young, just kids back then

Now we're older, can we try again?
Her laughter's like apples
Crisp and bright
I've never been so scared
Of something so right."

I pushed the curtains back and threw open the screen to lean out my window.

Justice caught my gaze, holding it as he continued to sing.

"I need her like the earth needs the rain
She's my sunshine after the pain
In her love, I find my way
As this chapter unfolds
We're a story written to last
So please
Stay with me."

I wanted to cry but my tears had vanished, replaced by joyful laughter that threatened to spill out and never stop.

He'd written me a song.

No.

He'd written *our* song.

"Daisies bloom where her feet touch the ground
Lost in her world, I'm finally found
Her touch is so gentle, like a summer breeze

In her arms, I find my ease.

We were lost, now we're found,
In each other, we're forever bound
Her voice is like a sweet melody
In her love, I find my sanctuary.

I need her like the earth needs the rain
She's my sunshine after the pain
In her love, I find my way
As this chapter unfolds
We're a story written to last
So please
Stay with me.

She's the girl next door,
My heart's desire
In her love, I'll never tire
With her, I've found my home
In her love, I'm never alone.

So please
Stay with me."

He finished the song and took off the guitar, discarding it on the grass.

"I love you, Hope Higgins," he called. "I love your kindness and your sass. I love your humor and how you pull me into line. I love your smiles and how they catalog each mood. I love how you're at once familiar and mysterious. And I want to spend the rest of my life uncovering every one of your mysteries."

I swallowed around the lump in my throat. "What about the books? And the allegations?"

"Nothing matters but us, baby. You can write all the smutty romance in the world and I'm gonna be proud as fuck of you for that. But I'm also going to insist in being involved in the research."

A laugh burst from me, tears beginning to flow once more.

"And as for the bullying, every single person who has ever met you knows that's untrue. You deserve better, baby. And we're gonna hold you tight and help you get through this."

He ducked his head for a beat before finding and holding my gaze once again.

"I left because I know I can't protect you from the media and people who would do anything to have their five minutes of fame. I thought leaving would be safer than staying—but it isn't. Cause I know deep in here"—he pumped a fist against his chest—"that we'll both be hurting for the rest of our lives if we don't give this a try."

I swiped at my tears impatiently. "What are you saying, Justice Wild?"

His lips curved into a grin so gorgeous my heart flipped.

"Be mine, Hope. Today, tomorrow, forever. Stay with me. Please."

I hesitated then stepped back from the window. "Gran?"

"Yes, dear?" I heard her call from the porch downstairs. No doubt she'd been there the entire time.

"Justice is sleeping over."

She cackled as he began to cross the yard, his long legs eating up the distance.

He climbed onto the roof and made it across to me in three quick strides. Without waiting to slip through the window, his hand snaked out to capture the back of my head and pull me into him. His lips captured mine in a hard and hungry kiss.

"I love you, Hope," he whispered. "I'm gonna be an ass time and time again, but don't give up on me. Please."

I cupped his face, brushing my thumb across his cheeks. "I love you." I pressed a chaste kiss to his nose. "Don't give up on me either. Deal?"

He grinned. "Deal."

We reached for each other's clothes at the same time, peeling the layers from our bodies.

"What's this?" I asked between kisses.

Justice had a bandage over his heart.

He stepped back, slowly peeling the dressing from his chest.

My breath caught, my heart flipping when I saw what he'd done.

"Justice…"

The blank space he'd reserved for his future partner had been filled. The dragon now cradled a book, the title of which read simply, *Hope*.

I traced the skin on either side of the tattoo, unable to believe he'd done this.

"What if I'd said no?"

"I took a chance," he whispered. "Knowing you're the only one who could ever take up this space."

I sighed. "You're such a romantic."

"Yeah?" He pulled me into him, pressing his lower body firmly against mine. "You gonna write some more smutty scenes about us?"

I grinned. "Maybe."

"Maybe?" he said, in mock outrage. He picked me up, striding to the bed. "Guess I better get to work inspiring you."

And with that, we began to write the next chapter of our beautiful life together.

16

HOPE

Song: ***Badass Woman*** **by Meghan Trainor**

Yes.

"You're sure about this?" Justice asked from his seat beside mine.

"Yep," I answered, clicking "add attachment" on the email.

"You don't have to do this if you're unsure."

I hit send on the email, sitting back in my chair with a satisfied sigh. "Too late now."

The past few weeks had been tumultuous. Justice had moved into the farmhouse with Gran and me after we'd broken his bed during a particularly vigorous morning.

I'd learned he hated mornings unless I woke him with my mouth around his cock, and he'd learned I needed space to write, or I became grumpy.... Unless I needed inspiration for a particularly steamy scene.

Our relationship had been marred with the weight of the bully allegations and the intense media scrutiny leveled our way—until yesterday. The shadow Ciara had cast over my life had been removed. The company had even released a public statement from the independent investigator noting that the allegations against me were baseless, a product of jealousy and ill intentions from a coworker who sought to tarnish my reputation for her own gain.

Justice had waged a full-on war against the tide of negative opinion, standing by my side throughout the whole ordeal and releasing statement after statement that proclaimed his support of me.

The full report hadn't been released publicly but reading through it I'd been struck by the avalanche of evidence of Ciara's vendetta against me. She'd wanted my job and had been willing to do anything she could to get it.

While the truth had come to light, the damage had been done, and I knew it was time to move on from this toxic environment.

It's time to follow my dreams.

"Hey."

I turned to look at Justice.

"Proud of you."

I shifted out of my chair to climb into his lap, straddling him as I wrapped my arms around his neck. "You do realize that this means I'm about to be unemployed."

He grinned. "I think you mean you're about to be a full-time author."

The words sounded sweet.

"Full-time author," I murmured, loving how they tasted on my tongue. "I'm living the dream."

He nuzzled into my neck, gently pressing slow kisses to my sensitive skin. "I have more good news."

I tilted my head to one side, granting him further access. "Mm?"

"The assisted living facility has an opening. Your Gran can move in at the end of the month."

My arms tightened around Justice as I pulled back to stare down at him. A future began to open before me, one I'd never considered.

"Justice... I...." Words failed me.

"Well, here's your next question," he said, shifting to catch my hand. From seemingly out of thin air a ring appeared. Slowly, he slid it onto my ring finger.

"The next leg of the tour kicks off next month," he said. "And I know you wanted to wait until Gran was settled, but with her moving out, I thought...."

I stared down at the unique ring, admiring the sapphires and diamonds that dotted the white gold band, turning my hand this way and that as they sparkled in the afternoon light.

I forced myself to look away from the gorgeous piece, barely able to believe this was happening.

"You thought?" I prompted, my heart in my throat.

He cupped my face, his thumb brushing gently over my cheek. "You might like to join me. Firstly, because all these destinations will give you more fodder for your next series. And secondly, we could get married in Italy." He leaned in to nibble a kiss across my lips. "And France." Another kiss. "And London." A third kiss. "And Australia." A fourth. "And—"

I caught his head in my hands, holding him still as I took over, pouring into the kiss all the joy and love I had for this amazing man.

"Yes, to all the adventures I can have with you," I whispered. "But we only really need one wedding."

"You sure? Cause I kind of like the idea of multiple wedding nights."

I giggled. "Of course, you do."

He chuckled then hauled himself up to a stand, holding me to him as he walked across to the bed. "Love you, Hope Higgins."

"And I love you, Justice Wild." I kissed him as he lowered us to the bed. "Now, make love to me."

"Yes, ma'am."

EPILOGUE 1

Justice
Songs:
Photograph **by Ed Sheeran**
Lucky **by Dermot Kennedy**

This is my favorite part

"Just so we're clear," Faye said, nodding toward the dance floor. "I was wrong."

I grinned, watching Hope with what I assumed had to be an unhealthy level of pride and possession.

"You're forgiven," I told her. "But only because I know you helped with her red dress moment."

She snorted. "Dude. You have no idea how much that cost me."

I raised my glass to her. "Then this is for your sacrifice," I tipped the soda bottle toward Hope. "It all worked out."

"Better than even I could imagine."

We watched our respective partners take the dance floor by storm, swinging and jiving in a way I could never even contemplate imitating.

"You ever look at Hope and wonder how you ended up together?" Faye asked, leaning her head on my shoulder.

"I don't have to wonder. Hope was always meant to be mine." I glanced down at her. "Do you?"

Faye tilted her head back, her gaze finding mine. "I have no idea how Sam and I came to be. We're so different and yet... we work."

I chuckled. "Oh, he orchestrated the fuck out of your fake wedding. Let's be honest. The boy had it bad for you years before you ever glanced at him."

"Same for you," she pointed out.

"True. Guess we're the idiots."

"I'll drink to that."

We clinked glasses.

The song finished and Sam and Hope separated, both laughing and flushed. Hope caught my eye, waving at me to come over.

With a beleaguered sigh, I pushed off the bar. "My wife calls."

"You're enjoying saying that far too much," Faye accused, straightening the cream-colored strap on her bridesmaid's dress.

"Oh, yeah."

By the time I'd made it onto the dance floor, the band had switched to a new song—a cover of *Lucky* by Dermot Kennedy.

Catching Hope around the waist, I pulled her into me, holding her tight.

"Come here, sweetheart," I murmured, beginning to sway with her. "I wanna hold you a minute."

She sighed, leaning into me. "Are you happy?"

"My cheeks hurt from grinning."

She giggled. "I love you."

"I love you too, baby." I cupped her cheek, brushing a thumb across her lips. "You are loved, Hope. This love inside me? It's scary how fucking much I love you."

She lifted on her toes to catch my lips in a sweet kiss that quickly turned hungry.

"Take me home," she whispered against my mouth. "I want you to make love to me in my wedding dress."

"As you wish."

Rearing back, I tossed my girl over my shoulder and carried her from the reception to the shouts and cheers of all the guests while   she—my   naughty   wife—cupped my ass.

I tossed her into my truck, grinning at her squeal.

"You ready?" I asked, sliding in beside her.

"For what?"

I started the truck. "You're the romance author. You tell me what happens next."

She caught my head in her hands, kissing me. "Oh, this is my favorite part."

"And that is?"

"Our happily ever after."

"Is that right?" I asked. "Then I guess we better get started."

Hope laughed, placing a hand on my knee. "But haven't we already?"

Catching her laughter with my mouth, I had to admit she was right.

We were living our happily ever after.

EPILOGUE 2

Justice
Sometime in the near future...
Song: *Blossom* by Dermot Kennedy

Dreams always come true

The guitar in my hand called to me, asking for a song I couldn't quite place. I plucked at the chords, listening absently as the notes blended with the sound of the waves that gently lapped the coastal shore.

I'd stolen my wife away for a week on a private island, far from photographers, fans and any other person except for the discreet staff at the resort.

Which meant we'd spent the first two days naked and in bed.

The only reason we were outside was because Hope had wanted to swim in the ocean, and I couldn't deny my wife anything.

"What's that?" Hope asked as she sat down beside me on the beach rug.

I shrugged. "Just something I'm fiddling with."

She nodded, leaning back on her elbows. "Do you think the world is okay with us being here?"

I snorted. "The world can fuck off. We need a break."

I wanted to reach for her, but the guitar seemed to jump under my hands, a song teasing at the edges of my consciousness.

Hope's cell rang, and she sighed heavily. "I know Faye said she'd call me later about the next leg of the tour and what I wanted to do but this is ridiculous."

I chuckled, knowing my gorgeous wife didn't actually mean that. If not for the fact I knew Faye loved Sam more than her life, I'd be worried she was making a move on my wife.

"Hey, can I call you—" Hope froze, her face blanking. A second later the phone dropped from her hand as she swallowed rapidly, turning blindly to me.

I tossed my guitar, pulling her in as I scooped the cell up.

"Talk," I barked at Faye. "What's happened?"

"SHE'S A NEW YORK TIMES BEST SELLER!" Faye screamed down the phone. "Your wife is on the charts!"

My fear snapped into elation.

"We'll call you back. Thanks." I tossed the phone and wrapped my arms around my sobbing wife, holding her close as she wept joyfully against me.

"So proud of you, Hope. I'm so fucking proud of you." I peppered her wet face with kisses, making her laugh.

"I'm overwhelmed. I'm okay, just overwhelmed."

"But happy?" I asked, already knowing the answer.

"Blissfully so." She sighed and leaned into me. "Is this a dream?"

"Probably." I guided her down to the rug. "But dreams always come true, don't you know?"

Her smile held my heart. "I know. You're proof of that."

I reached for the straps on her bikini. "How about we celebrate your milestone, hmm?"

She chuckled. "I love you."

I paused in my efforts to remove her clothes. "I love you too, Hope. Always."

She kissed me gently then pushed my head down her body. "Now get to work."

"Your wish is my command."

It always would be, because she was my wildest Hope.

Thank you for reading Justice and Hope's story!
Want more?
Check out their bonus epilogue via my website
EvieMitchell.com

ABOUT EVIE MITCHELL

Evie Mitchell is a thirty-something romance author (she/her/hers) who loves tales of fierce romance.
She lives with a chronic illness and often writes disability-inclusive romance.

Her loves include steamy romance novels, her husband, their sausage dogs (heaven help her), and her ever-growing collection of book-related mugs.

You can catch up with Evie on all socials at @EvieMitchellAuthor

Visit Evie's website for her current booklist
www.EvieMitchell.com